The social worker brushed Con's words aside. "If *indeed* you are his father, you'd be a single father at best. I'm sorry, Mr. Randolph, but you can't expect to convince the court that the child would be better off with you than with a normal loving family."

"You're talking about love, ma'am," Robyn said, jumping in. "How can you possibly measure the love a father has for his son?"

"Just what, exactly, is your relationship with Mr. Randolph?" the woman asked.

"Like Con told you, we're childhood friends."

"Too bad. He'd at least have a chance of convincing the courts to take him seriously if he got married."

Robyn's gaze flew to Con's face, and he couldn't believe what her eyes were telling him.... Surely even Robbie wouldn't go so far as to tie herself to a loveless marriage to help him out. As for him... marriage? To Robbie? There was no way. She was his best friend. His only friend.

Marry Robbie? No way in hell.

ABOUT THE AUTHOR

Tara Taylor Quinn worked as a journalist and an English teacher before she finally realized her dream of becoming a Harlequin writer—a dream she'd nursed ever since buying her first Harlequin Romance novel at the age of fourteen. Tara makes her home in Arizona with her husband and daughter.

Tara loves to hear from her readers. You can reach her at P.O. Box 15065, Scottsdale, Arizona 85267-5065 or on-line at http://www.inficad.com/~ttquinn.

Books by Tara Taylor Quinn

HARLEQUIN SUPERROMANCE
567—YESTERDAY'S SECRETS
584—McGILLUS V. WRIGHT
600—DARE TO LOVE
624—NO CURE FOR LOVE
661—JACOB'S GIRLS
696—THE BIRTH MOTHER
729—ANOTHER MAN'S CHILD

Don't miss any of our special offers. Write to us at the following address for information on our newest releases.

Harlequin Reader Service
U.S.: 3010 Walden Ave., P.O. Box 1325, Buffalo, NY 14269
Canadian: P.O. Box 609, Fort Erie, Ont. L2A 5X3

SHOTGUN BABY
Tara Taylor Quinn

Harlequin Books

TORONTO • NEW YORK • LONDON
AMSTERDAM • PARIS • SYDNEY • HAMBURG
STOCKHOLM • ATHENS • TOKYO • MILAN
MADRID • WARSAW • BUDAPEST • AUCKLAND

ISBN 0-373-70750-9

SHOTGUN BABY

Printed in U.S.A.

For Joni Knox Pepperell
whose friendship stood the test of time
in spite of the odds

PROLOGUE

SOMEBODY'S WITH HIM. Con took another swallow of whiskey, trying to drown the memory of the sergeant's words.

They'd had to go in. They'd been out of time. As soon as Nick Ramirez heard about the bust he'd have vanished. And they'd have been back to square one. Again. The drugs would be on the streets and kids would be dying.

Somebody's with him.

He lit a cigarette and motioned for another drink. "Make it a double."

The bartender grunted.

Con paid for the drink, downed it quickly and slid his empty glass back across the scarred wood of the bar. "Again," he said.

Hell, he wasn't the one who'd screwed up. He wasn't the one who'd panicked, who'd arrested members of Ramirez's organization before Ramirez himself had been brought in. One thing Special Agent Connor Randolph did not do was panic. Ever.

Somebody's with him.

Con shook his head. The words wouldn't leave him

alone. "Another one," he said, concentrating on his enunciation. "Better start a tab."

How could he have known? Hell, anyone in the same room as Ramirez had to smell as rank as he did. The slimy lawyer had been stinking up Phoenix for years. But they hadn't nailed him on drugs; check fraud was the charge they'd finally been able to hang on him. And they'd been damn lucky to do that. Ramirez filled his organization with his own kind, and they stuck together.

Somebody's with him.

Con tipped the whiskey glass to his mouth again. So somebody was with Ramirez. Two for the price of one, he'd thought. A deal.

A deal. The somebody with him was a woman. A young blond beauty. Wearing a blue dress. Con squeezed his eyes shut, but that didn't obliterate the images that tormented him. How much more alcohol was it going to take?

"May I sit down?"

Opening his eyes, he slowly turned toward the voice. Could it be her?

"May I?" she asked a second time.

He nodded and the woman took the stool beside his. It sure looked like her. The alcohol was finally working.

"How come you're all alone?" she asked.

He shrugged and glanced at her. At least she wasn't

wearing blue. His cigarette had burned itself out in the ashtray and he lit a new one.

"I'm all alone, too," she said. "I don't like being alone. Do you?"

He shook his head. "Buy you a drink?"

Of course, he could understand why she'd changed her dress. Red splotches had messed up the blue one.

"Sure, if you want to. A glass of wine, please," she told the bartender. "Red."

That could have been what was spilled all over her pretty blue dress. Red wine. There was something drastically wrong with this theory, but he didn't have the energy to figure out what. Con sipped his drink, welcoming oblivion.

"You don't mind if I sit here, do you? I'm not bothering you or anything?"

Hell no, she wasn't bothering him. She'd just saved him from his demons. He shook his head again.

"It's just…I didn't want to be alone, but when I came in here, most of the men looked at me like I was good for only one thing, you know what I mean? But *you* didn't. You don't see me like that, do you?"

To tell the truth, Con couldn't see her clearly at all. The lighting in the bar wasn't that great to begin with, and things were getting blurrier by the minute. He gave her his standard answer, a shake of the head. It was just about all he could manage. It seemed to satisfy her.

"I guess you broke your nose sometime, huh? It's

okay, though. I like the rugged look. How about you? What do you like?"

Con shrugged. He couldn't think of anything at the moment. He lit another cigarette.

"You sure are big, even for a man. I mean I can see you're in fantastic shape, but I don't know if I've ever sat beside such a big man. You're sitting down and all, but there's hardly room for your legs under the bar."

Con nodded.

"I know I chatter a lot. Does it bother you? I can leave you alone if you want."

"No!" Anything but that. As long as he didn't question things too deeply, she was keeping the demons at bay. He needed her to stay right there beside him. "Don't go." And then, just to make certain, he added, "Please."

"Sure. Don't worry. I'll stay. For as long as you like. I got no place to be. You got someplace to be?"

He didn't want to think about life outside the bar or even off the stool. "Nope."

"So, whatcha wanna talk about?"

He shrugged, took a drag on his cigarette. Talking meant thinking, didn't it? He didn't want to talk.

"That's okay. I can do most of the talking if you want. It won't hurt my feelings if you just wanna sit there. I know what. You want me to tell you the story about how my dog—Estelle, that was her name—you want me to tell you how Estelle got into the movies?"

A dog in the movies. "Sure," he said. She wanted to tell him about a dog in the movies. Nobody had ever talked to him about dogs in movies.

Slouched silently beside her, he half listened to her ramblings, smoking his cigarettes and drinking his whiskey. As long as she kept talking he was going to be all right.

"I have a cat now. They're so much more independent, know what I mean? How about you? You got a cat?"

"Nope." No cat would want to live with him.

"You should get one. They're lots better than living alone."

Con wasn't so sure. He liked living alone. Most of the time. It was a helluva lot better than just making do with someone or knowing that someone was just making do with you. Alone meant there was no one around to disappoint.

"You do live by yourself, don't you? I mean you aren't wearing a ring or nothing, not that all men do even these days, but if you were married or, like, had someone, you wouldn't be sitting here all alone on a Friday night, right?"

What? Con was having difficulty concentrating. He nodded, because that seemed to be the response she wanted, and raised his glass to his lips once more.

"Me, too, I been living alone for a whole week, ever since that rat Joe threw me out," she said. "And all because I like to watch the soaps. Lotsa wives watch the soaps, and even though we weren't married yet, I was sure we would be, so keeping house and watching the soaps was a real job even if Joe said it wasn't.''

Something pricked at Con's conscience. "What about your son?" he asked. His tongue felt like it had doubled in size.

"My son? I don't have a son."

He looked at her, but couldn't quite focus. "You sure?" They'd said she had a fifteen-year-old kid.

"I'm sure. I don't have *any* children, even though I'm almost twenty-seven. I haven't even been married.''

So they'd been wrong about her kid. He felt like crying with relief. And she hadn't been married, either. He drained his glass to celebrate.

"You mind if I have another drink?" the woman asked.

"Have whatever you want." He owed it to her.

"Really? Like, I can get a burger, too? You want something to eat?"

Con's stomach churned. There'd been a half-eaten burger on the desk that afternoon. "No." He just needed another drink.

She ordered her food and a carafe of wine. He was glad she planned to stay around a bit longer. Maybe after a while he'd get himself some food.

"I bet you have a job. An important one, too, just like Joe. He owns ice-cream shops and he wears a suit to work every day. You just get off work? That why you're still in your suit?"

He'd changed suits. The one he'd put on that morning had been soaked with blood.

"Don't get me wrong. I think it's great you're still wearing your suit. I like men in suits."

With painfully clear vision, Con saw a man in a suit. A dark-haired man wearing a light gray suit. A man who put a gun to an innocent woman's head and held it there, fully intending to blow her brains out if Con didn't get out of his way and let him go free—

"You okay, mister?"

"Huh?" Turning to look at the woman beside him, Con found his focus blessedly blurry again. "Fine."

"I didn't mean to turn you off by saying I liked you in your suit. I'm not after you or anything. At least, not unless you want me to be. But it can only be for tonight, anyway, because I've already got a date for tomorrow night. And he's a really nice guy. I met him standing in line at the bank. It was kind of funny, really. I've only ever been with Joe, and there I was cashing the check that Joe gave me when he kicked me out, and I meet someone else. Life's weird, huh? Anyway, I'll just move down a seat if you want."

"No! No. Stay." He gulped the last of his drink. *Please, God. Make her stay. Let her be okay for a while longer.* Let him pretend...

The woman in the blue dress had been in Nick

Ramirez's office to do some redecorating. She'd had no connection to the lawyer's organization at all. She'd been clean, innocent. And her perfume had lingered in the air even after the gun had gone off when she'd tried to pull away from Ramirez.

"You sad about something, mister? You keep getting a funny look on your face."

Her concern pulled Con back from the abyss. She was sitting beside him. Healthy and alive. He'd never been more grateful for the presence of another human being in his life. "I'm fine," he said, because there was nothing else he could say.

She ran her fingers along the back of his hand. He was almost too numb to feel the light contact, but he saw the whiteness of her skin against his. There was a gentle quality to her touch, something Con had known little of in his life. The only person who'd ever shown him any gentleness at all, and only when she thought he wasn't looking, was Robbie, and he couldn't think about her right now. She was going to be pissed off that he hadn't called her. She always got first dibs on the story when he closed a case.

The woman patted his hand.

"You shouldn't do that," he felt compelled to tell her. "Might get dirty." But he didn't pull away.

"I'll wash my hands." She giggled.

Yeah. If you got dirty, you could wash. Maybe he just needed to wash.

Her burger arrived and she ate as if she hadn't had

a meal in days. He was glad she was enjoying herself. He didn't have to feel so guilty for needing her to stay beside him.

"You want dessert?" he asked. Anything to prolong her visit, to keep the truth at bay.

"Sure, if you don't mind."

"Have whatever you want." It took all his concentration to form a coherent sentence. His head was swimming, his brain muddled. Another drink or two and he'd stumble next door where the pink neon motel sign was blinking, to the room he'd rented. Just as soon as he was sure the voice in his head wouldn't follow him there.

An hour passed. Then two.

"It's time to close up." Con didn't like the bartender's tone of voice. It reminded him of another warning.

Somebody's with him.

The images assaulted him again. He shook his head and looked at the woman beside him. Her eyes were awash with fear. The look was too familiar, and he knew he had to make her fear go away. He had to get it right this time.

"Wha's wrong?" he asked her.

"I don't wanna go home. I've only been living alone for a week and I get scared at night."

He reached out an unsteady hand, intending to stroke her hair. His hand landed around her shoulder, instead. "You don' have to be scared."

"It's just that I never knew how thin the walls of a trailer are. I can hear every sound, every car that drives by, and I lie there all stiff until I'm sure it's passed. Joe won't let me in at home. But I don't wanna go back to the trailer he bought me, not when it's dark out."

Con took another look at the woman beside him. *A second chance.* He had to help her before it was too late.

"You can come with me if you want," he heard himself offer, although he had no idea what he'd do with her if she did. He could hardly entertain a woman when he was passed out on a motel bed.

"Can I? You really don't mind?"

The fear was fading from her eyes. He'd saved the day, after all. "Sure," he said, leaning on her just a little as he slid off his stool and threw several bills down from the wad in his money clip. He pulled the motel key from his pocket and stumbled out of the bar, then across the parking lot beside his guardian angel. The night air cooled his skin, lessening his stupor, allowing the dark images to fill his mind once again. It didn't hit him until they were inside the motel room and she flipped on the light. Something was very wrong. A reason this woman couldn't make anything better.

She wasn't the same blonde who was haunting him. She couldn't possibly be.

Somebody's with him.

"She died." His words cracked like a gunshot in the tiny room.

Coming out of the bathroom, a bar of soap in her hand, she said, "Who died?"

Pain exploded through Con's head. He sank down on the side of the bed, burying his head in his hands to try to still the pounding.

"Who died?" Her soft voice wafted across him, as feather light as her hand on the back of his neck.

"I tried to get to her, to stop him, but there was no time. She stumbled when she pulled away, and the gun went off."

She snatched her hand back. "You killed someone?"

"No!" He couldn't stand the accusation in her voice. It was too much like the echo in his head. "I'm the good guy." At least that was what he'd been in the beginning. He wasn't sure when all that changed, when getting his man became the most important thing.

"You're a cop?" Even through his alcohol-fuzzed mind he heard the hope in her voice.

"Yeah," he said. Sort of. He had a license to carry a gun.

"Well, it's okay, then." The soothing touch returned to his neck. "You were only doing your job."

And what exactly was that? To make the bust? To close the case? Or to protect the innocent? The hammers were pounding so fiercely in his head he couldn't be sure of anything.

Except that as the woman sat down beside him, as her fingers continued to caress him, the vision of blood soiling a pretty blue dress faded just a little.

"Here, let's get you out of this jacket, OK? And loosen your tie. There, that's better, isn't it? Now just lie down here and I'll rub your back. Joe used to love it when I rubbed his back."

Before he realized it, Con found himself stretched out on the bed, his angel of mercy sitting beside him working magic on his tortured muscles. When he was sober enough to think, he was going to make this up to her. Somehow he would find a way to thank her for saving him.

But when he awoke late the next morning, alone, naked and sick as a dog, the only thing to tell that she'd been there was an empty money clip, and his FBI badge lying open on the table beside it.

Holding the badge, looking toward the unmade bed, he hoped to God he hadn't done anything else to hate himself for. The last thing he remembered was a woman's cool hand running gently along his back, and him wanting to thank her for something. But he couldn't thank her. He didn't even know her name.

CHAPTER ONE

Fifteen months later

IT WAS DONE. And done right. He should care.

"Congratulations, Randolph."

Con nodded at FBI Special Agent Orlando and continued on his way out of the bowels of the Tyler building in downtown Phoenix. Orlando's job was just beginning; he had cleanup detail—documenting every shred of evidence so that when operation Dogtags came to trial the government could nail these bastards.

"You did it again, Randolph. Thanks." Maricopa County Sheriff Tom Whitcomb was standing just inside the front door of the building with a couple of his men, waiting for William Tyler to appear.

Con nodded again, shoved his hands into the pockets of his slacks and headed silently out into the blistering June heat. The sun felt good. He barely noticed the flashing lights of the police cruisers surrounding the area. After fifteen years with the FBI very little fazed him.

"I'll get you for this, Randolph!"

Con turned just in time to see William Tyler make a complete ass of himself as he was escorted out of the building that, until today, had been an institution, a monument to the Tyler dynasty in Phoenix. William Tyler, the epitome of the American dream, a classic case of a good man making good. He'd been a poor itinerant preacher who'd started with one small investment. And he'd donated his first million to the church. The sedately suited man was hollering loudly enough to be heard on the next block. "I'll hunt you down and cut your—"

Con turned his back. He'd really expected the man to go quietly with a measure of class. During the past several months of investigation, he'd found Tyler to be a crook, but a gentleman just the same.

Or maybe he'd just wanted to find something good in the ex-preacher. Something redeemable in one of the shady characters he dealt with day after day, year after year. What he'd found, instead, was a foul-mouthed villain.

Con lowered himself into his nondescript sedan, government-issue blue, and cursed as his knee hit the dash. Turning his key in the ignition and setting the air conditioner to high, he reached for his cell phone and the cigarettes on the console at the same time. He dialed first.

"Newsroom." Her voice was like a welcome blast of fresh air.

"OK, Robbie," he said, pulling a cigarette from his pack. "It's public now. It's Tyler."

"William Tyler? *He's* the investment broker you've been after?"

Con took a long satisfying drag on his cigarette. "He's on his way downtown now."

"This is good news."

"Uh-huh."

"So how come you sound so whipped? What's the matter with you, Randolph?"

Trust Robbie to jump right into his personal minefield. Nobody else would dare talk to him like that. Nobody else would get away with it. "It's just a job."

"It didn't used to be." Her voice was soft, unusually tender. "I'm worried about you."

Yeah. Lately he was getting a little worried himself. "Don't be. Now get your butt down here or you'll lose an exclusive."

"I'm on my way."

The phone was almost back in its holder when Con heard Robbie call his name.

"Yeah?"

"Take care, friend."

TWO HOURS LATER Robyn Blair was back at the TV station. She'd just spent the afternoon covering the arrest of one of Phoenix's pillars of society, a man who'd been charged with insider trading. Tyler had a beautiful wife of thirty-five years, three great kids, all college graduates, a couple of grandchildren and was an ordained minister. Go figure.

She was looking forward to a nice cold beer in a frosted mug. Hearing voices coming from the newsroom at the end of the hall, she prepared to join the guys for their Wednesday-night jaunt to Coyote's.

"Come on, let's get going. Robbie may not be back for hours," she heard Tom Richards, a staff writer for the six-o'clock news, say. "I think maybe she's gone back to police headquarters."

"I'm ready," Darrin Michaels boomed. He was one of Channel Four's star photographers. "Going without Robbie might be nice for a change. At least I won't have Alysse harping at me when I get home. Why that woman has a problem with Robbie joining us for a beer I'll never know."

"You, too? I thought Joan was the only one who had a screw loose where Robbie's concerned."

Robbie stopped in her tracks as Rick Hastings, her producer, jumped into the conversation. Joan had a problem with Rick having drinks with her? She couldn't believe it! Hell, she'd baby-sat their kids just last weekend so Joan and Rick could go to the movies. Joan had said she didn't know what they'd do without her.

"Connie, too." That was Tom again. *Connie, too?* Robbie sagged back against the wall, her notebook hugged against her chest. She'd considered all three

of those women her friends. How could they not have
faith in her—or in their husbands? It was ludicrous.

"I don't get it. It's not like I'd be interested in
Robbie even if I were free," Tom continued.

Robbie was glad to hear it.

"Me, either," Darrin seconded. "If you took her
dancing, she'd probably want to lead."

"I wouldn't go that far, but Robbie is a bit too
aggressive for my taste," said Rick.

Rick's words hit her harder, probably because he
was right. But a woman in her profession *had* to be
aggressive.

"It's not just that she has the tenacity of a pit
bull," Tom added. "Can you guys honestly say you'd
ever want to get into bed with a woman whose hair
is as short as yours and who wouldn't know what to
do with a tube of makeup if she had one? I'll bet she
even wears boxer shorts for underwear."

The other guys laughed.

Robbie had never been overly fond of Tom Richards, and she was liking him less and less. Short hair
was easy to manage. And so what if she'd never understood why smearing goop on her face was supposed to be a good thing; at least, she'd been blessed
with a complexion that didn't need any covering up.
And she most certainly did not wear boxer shorts.

"And she'd insist on being on top all the time,
too," Darrin added, causing another round of male
laughter. Robbie stood frozen outside the door. She'd

thought these guys were her pals! But she had to admit—in her one brief relationship, she *had* rather enjoyed being on top.

"Come on, guys, Robbie's all right," Rick said. "Besides, have you ever taken a look at her legs? They're the best pair I've seen since Christy Brinkley's. I can tell you, under different circumstances, I wouldn't mind having them wrapped around me."

"Yeah, but only if the package was different."

Robbie didn't know whether to slink away quietly or to barge into the room and strangle Tom Richards with her aggressive hands.

"Oh, I don't know, her boobs aren't so bad, either," Darrin said. "Come to think of it, when you get past the way she acts and dresses, her body's worth taking a second look at."

"And a third."

Robbie gritted her teeth at the newly appreciative tone in Tom's voice.

"OK, guys, we better go have that drink before we get ourselves in too deep to pretend we never had this conversation," Rick said, suddenly serious. "Robbie is Robbie, aggression and all, and she's saved our butts more than once. Let's just hope she never learns how to shop for clothes, or our wives'd really start harping. And I don't know about you, but if I'm going to be nagged, I'd just as soon it be over someone who turned me on."

The men approached the door and Robbie slipped

into the women's room across the hall. She'd never been so thankful to find the place empty in her life. It would have been the last straw to have had to explain the tears streaming down her cheeks.

As Con pulled into his driveway that evening, he saw a woman at his front door. Which would have been fine with him if his professional eye hadn't already cataloged her in detail. This was not one of his occasional female acquaintances.

This woman had to be pushing sixty. Her posture was stiff and her clothing prim. With that manila folder clutched in her fingers, she looked just like his fourth-grade English teacher, old sourpuss McLaughlin. He had no idea who she was, and he wasn't in the mood to find out. It didn't appear, however, that he'd have much choice. She'd seen him pull into the driveway.

Opening his automatic garage door, Con drove inside and closed the door behind him. When he entered the kitchen, he dropped his keys on the ceramic-tiled counter, pulled a beer from the refrigerator, uncapped it and took a swig. With his free hand he picked up the pack of cigarettes he'd left on the counter that morning. One long satisfying drag later he walked, beer in hand, to his front door and swung it open. "Yes?"

The woman's face took on an even more sour look

as she appraised Con. "Are you Mr. Connor Randolph?"

"Who wants to know?" he asked, purposely allowing his cigarette to hang out of the corner of his mouth. He'd had to put up with snobs like her throughout his adolescence, but he wasn't a kid anymore.

He leaned against the doorjamb, allowing himself the satisfaction of forcing her to take a step backward. He was always conscious of his intimidating stature **an**d normally tried not to take unfair advantage of it unless he was working, but at the moment he didn't give a damn about fair.

"The state wants to know."

The state? He was the state.

Flicking the ashes of his cigarette outside the door, he took another long drag. What he really wanted was to finish his beer, strip off his clothes and dive into his backyard pool.

"You collecting money or signatures?" he asked, resigned to giving her either so she'd go away and leave him alone.

"Are you Connor Randolph?" she repeated.

Stepping back, he nodded.

"Then if I could just get your signatures here, I'll be on my way." She pulled some forms from her folder and thrust them at his chest.

Con stubbed his cigarette in the hallway ashtray and reached into his suit jacket for his pen. "What is it this time—higher taxes or better neighborhoods?" he asked, barely glancing at the papers. If she wanted something from him, she sure wasn't going about it the right way. But then, it was probably hard to get people to go door-to-door collecting signatures anymore.

"It's your son, Mr. Randolph." She practically spit the words.

He froze, his pen poised above the papers. "What did you say?"

"Your son. We've found a family who wants to adopt your son. A fine proper family. The only thing holding us up now is your signature. So if you could just sign these preliminary forms, we can get the formal proceedings under way. Of course, the state will also be petitioning you for child support for the three months he's been with us."

Con lowered his pen. "I don't have a son."

She didn't bat an eye. "My name is Sandra Muldoon, Mr. Randolph. I work for social services. And according to our records, you do have a son. Now if you could just sign there on the line marked with a star—"

Con's back was suddenly as stiff as hers. "I don't have a son."

"I realize you refused responsibility for the child, Mr. Randolph, but that doesn't negate his existence. However, we're prepared to sever all connections just as you wish. You need only to sign the forms."

She had the wrong man. Con had no interest in having a child, in fact had decided quite unequivocally that he would never bring a child into such an ugly world. But neither would he refuse responsibility for one he'd created. Not ever. This woman had the wrong man.

"Who's the mother?" he asked.

"Cecily Barnhardt," she said, as if he already knew full well who the mother was and was wasting her time.

It was all the confirmation Con needed. "I've never heard of her."

The woman's mouth fell open. "Never heard of her? Well—" the scorn was back in her voice "—I must say you might at least try to learn the names of the women you, uh, consort with in the future, Mr. Randolph, especially if you aren't going to consort responsibly. Now, if you'll just sign these forms..."

Con turned to the hall table and set down the beer he'd been holding. Hard. It foamed up and over the mouth of the bottle. "I've never 'consorted,' nor had sex, with a Cecily Barnhardt," he said, enunciating very clearly, though softly, as he reached to close the door in the woman's face.

"She says you did. And we have proof."

He pulled the door back open and glared.

"It's all right here." She shook the manila folder in front of his face. "The baby was conceived at the Pink Lagoon Motel the night of March sixteenth last year. In room 173—a room registered to you. He was born at Phoenix Baptist Hospital on December twentieth and abandoned at the same hospital three months later with his birth certificate and a letter from his mother begging that someone give him a good home. You, sir, are the father named on the birth certificate.''

Con felt the blood drain from his face. Anyone could be named on a birth certificate. He knew that.

But he had been at the Pink Lagoon. He'd never forget that seedy motel. Or, no matter how hard he tried, that date. Just as he'd never remember what did or did not happen after he'd reached his motel room the night he'd deliberately drunk himself into a stupor.

"Now, if you will just sign these papers…'' The woman said again.

"No.'' Nausea roiled inside of him.

"Excuse me?''

"No.'' He couldn't be much clearer than that.

"But you said you didn't want to have anything to do with the child.''

"I said nothing of the kind.''

"It's all here, Mr. Randolph. We found Cecily and she told us how she couldn't care for the child herself and that the baby's father had refused to help her. She signed him over to the state.''

Con stood to his full six-foot-five height. "Let's understand one thing. I would never have turned my back on a child of mine if I'd had any idea that it existed. If, as you say, this child is mine, *I* will take him. *I* will raise him," he insisted—though he had no idea how he could possibly do such a thing. He knew only that he couldn't *not* do it.

"But you can't!"

Her reaction didn't surprise him. He'd been getting it all his life.

"Can't I?"

Her gaze raked him, stopping for pointed moments on beer splattered on the hall table. "Well, look at you. You can't possibly care for a baby."

He felt as if he were back in the seventh grade and his teacher was telling him he couldn't possibly expect to run for class president. He was, after all, nothing but a troublemaker, a loser.

"*Is* the child mine?" His steely gray eyes held her gaze.

"Y-yes. It would appear so. But—"

"Then *I* will care for him. Where is he?" Con looked behind her, almost as if he expected the child to appear.

"He's in a foster home in Gilbert, but—"

"Then let's go get him," he said.

"You can't just go get him!" Sandra Muldoon cried, shocked.

"Of course I can. He's mine."

"Th-there will have to be tests. We'll need proof. Besides, you can't really mean to raise him yourself."

"Why not?" The more she pushed him, the more desperate he became to rescue his son from the same system that had made his own childhood such a mockery.

"You aren't even married!"

"There's no law against that." Finally, something in the whole mess he was sure about.

"But you can't—" She broke off when Con's gaze turned steely again. "This is highly unexpected," she said.

"I want my son."

Putting the forms back into her folder, she clutched it to her chest. "Yes, well, there will be procedures."

"Such as?" Procedures. Something he was used to.

"Blood tests, for one."

"But you said he's my son. You're not sure?"

"One can never be certain about these things."

"You were certain enough when you wanted my signature to give him away. And certain enough to take my money for his back support."

"There will have to be blood tests, Mr. Randolph. We can't just hand over an innocent baby—"

"Not even to his father?" The words made him quiver inside.

"He's a ward of the state now," she said, as if that changed the child's parentage.

"So I'll get a blood test. Where can I pick him up?"

"I'm telling you, Mr. Randolph, you can't just go

get him. We'll have to send someone from social services over first.''

''Why?''

Her eyes grew wide. ''To see if you're a fit father of course!''

''And you do this every time people give birth?''

''No,'' she said impatiently. ''But you chose not to be present when Cecily gave birth.''

''I wasn't informed she was pregnant.''

Mrs. Muldoon didn't look like she believed him. ''You also chose not to support him when she came to you asking for help.''

''She never came.''

''She says she did,'' the social worker snipped, still clutching her folder. ''And which of you is telling the truth is something for the courts to decide. In the meantime, if you're serious about this, you'll need to call this number to set up an appointment with social services.'' She handed him a business card and turned haughtily, her back ramrod straight as she headed out to her car, parked at the curb.

''Wait a minute,'' Con called. But he wasn't sure what he wanted to say when she turned back to him, her eyebrows raised in irritation.

''He's normal, isn't he?'' he asked, suddenly scared to death that there might be something wrong with his son, something he couldn't fix.

''Does it make a difference to your wanting him?'' Her voice was like an icicle dripping down his spine.

Of course she'd believe the worst of him. "No."

"He's perfectly normal, Mr. Randolph. And happy, too, for that matter. He's been well cared for. And will continue to be well cared for if he's adopted. I suggest you think long and hard before you decide to change the course of his young life. Even if you succeed in this foolishness, what could you possibly give him that would make up for his losing his rightful place in the bosom of a loving family?"

Con never moved a muscle as she delivered her last verbal slap, then strode to her car, climbed in and sped away.

Long minutes later he shut his front door, went into the living room and fell onto the couch.

He had a son. *My God, he had a son.*

CHAPTER TWO

HE WAS STILL HALF LYING there, holding the telephone receiver in his hand and staring off into space when Robbie burst through his front door an hour later.

"Hey, what's with the beer here?" she called by way of greeting.

When she didn't get an answer, she picked up the bottle from the front-hall table, took a swig and choked. "Yuck! How long's that been sitting there? I can't get a cold beer tonight to save my soul."

It was then that she looked into the living room and noticed Con on the couch. His face was ashen, his gaze vacant. "Hey, what's wrong?" she asked, her heart pounding in fright as she came in. "What happened?"

"I have a son." He didn't even look at her.

She stopped in her tracks, feeling the shock of his words all the way to her toes. She must have heard him wrong.

"You have a son," she repeated. This was some kind of cruel joke, just like the conversation she'd overheard at the station. It had to be.

"Yeah." His vacant gaze slid over her as he finally hung up the phone. "*I* have a son. Kinda hard to get used to, huh?"

She stared at him, seeing the truth in his shell-shocked eyes. She'd always told herself this day would come. When she'd be faced with the final evidence of Con's love for a woman who wasn't her. But she'd expected to have survived the pain of his marriage first.

"Who's his mother?"

She prayed that Con wouldn't notice the jealousy in her voice. He'd never had any idea how she felt about him. And she intended to keep it that way.

He shrugged. "Cecily something or other."

"You don't *know?*" Con's flings were always premeditated. He was never careless, would never allow the possibility of repercussions.

"It was that night at the Pink Lagoon." He said the words so softly she barely caught them. And suddenly she understood.

"I thought you said nothing happened." She stood in the middle of the living room, her arms wrapped around herself.

"I hoped nothing had. I can't remember."

Her heart twisted inside out, her limbs as weak as her stomach had suddenly become. She was a tough woman. She could handle anything. So why was she falling apart at the seams?

And why, if he was going to make love and not remember it, couldn't it have been with her?

"So that makes him what, five, six months old?" she asked, still unable to convince herself the child was real. *She* was the one who craved parenthood, not Con.

"Six months tomorrow, the twentieth. He was born December twentieth."

She sank onto the opposite end of the couch before her legs gave out on her. Con even knew the birthdate.

"So, are you going to see his mother?" She detested the woman, everything about her.

Con glanced at Robbie. "I don't know."

She couldn't hold his gaze, couldn't trust herself to hide the tumult of emotions raging inside her. She loved him. She hurt for him—and for his child. She hurt for herself. Her worst nightmare had always been losing Con.

"Don't you think you should?" She could barely get the words past her lips.

"I didn't even know her name until an hour ago. Besides, she doesn't have the kid."

"Then who does?"

"He's in a foster home at the moment."

Oh, God. Her heart filled with the same hopeless desperation she'd felt as a teenager trying to understand the unfairness in Con's life. She knew there were some wonderful foster homes, some children who lived better lives because of loving foster parents, but Con only knew what could go *wrong* with the system. He'd grown up in a foster home. Right next door to her. He'd lived with people who called him their son but never adopted him because of the support they would lose from the state for his care. And they'd never let him forget that he should be grateful to them for taking him, someone else's bastard, either.

He'd always hated his biological parents for subjecting him to that, for not standing by him, and had always sworn he'd never do the same to any kid of his.

Just one more reason to hate himself.

"What's his name?" she asked.

Con looked at her blankly for a moment. "I don't know," he finally said.

She ached to hold him.

"I didn't even think to ask," he added, as if he was lower than dirt.

"So you'll ask."

Con has a son. A baby. It was suddenly frighteningly real. And maybe even a bit exciting.

"How soon can you see him?" *And can I go with you?*

He shrugged. "It's not that simple." Reaching into his jacket pocket, he pulled out an empty cigarette pack, tossed it, then grabbed a new pack from the end table. He opened it, shook out a cigarette and lit it.

Robbie waited.

"He's a ward of the state," he finally said. "I have to go through social services."

"Even to see him?"

He took a long drag on the cigarette. "Apparently."

Even back when she'd first met Con, he'd been a boy of few words, having already learned not to trust his thoughts and feelings to those around him. But if she'd done nothing else in the twenty-five years since, she'd proved to him that she was the one person in the world he could count on.

She took his cigarette from his fingers and had a puff, then put it out. She was trying to get him to quit.

"Talk to me, Randolph," she said.

He lit another cigarette. "Want a beer?" He was off the couch and heading for the kitchen, taking his pack of cigarettes with him.

What she wanted was for him to stop shutting her out. "Sure." She followed him to the kitchen and sat on a stool at the ceramic-tiled breakfast bar.

Con grabbed two beers from the refrigerator and joined her, dropping his cigarette in the ashtray on the bar. Robbie picked it up, took another puff and put it out.

"I want my son." The words were raw, shattering the silence.

She resisted the urge to reach for his hand and hold

it, a form of comfort she knew he wouldn't accept. "Of course you do," she said, raising her bottle and taking a swallow of the cold brew.

He lit another cigarette. "I want to raise him," he said, his look challenging.

"OK." If he'd hoped to shock her, he'd failed. That he'd want to be a father to his child didn't surprise her in the least.

"I'm not father material." The stark words hung between them.

"Baloney." She eyed his cigarette, but took a sip of her beer, instead.

"That social worker, Mrs. Muldoon, couldn't have made her horror at the thought of my raising the child plainer," he said, his voice low. "When she arrived I had a cigarette hanging out of my mouth, a beer in my hand, and I'd just come away from a man who was threatening to cut off my balls."

Robbie smiled. "You don't need 'em, Randolph, you already made the kid."

Con didn't return her smile. He took another swallow of beer, then proceeded to scrape off the label with his thumb. "I should've answered the door before getting the beer."

"Lots of fathers have an occasional beer. Ever since you've been old enough to drink, you've been drunk a total of one time. I hardly think anybody can condemn you for that."

He shrugged.

"And besides, since when do they do a character check before allowing a man to see his son?"

"Since the state only wants a man to give the kid away."

"They what? To whom?"

Con shrugged again. "There's a family…"

"Why would they look for a family to take him without consulting his father first?"

"They're under the impression I already knew about the child and refused support." He pushed the beer-label scraps into a neat pile.

"Why would they think that?"

"Cecily said so."

None of this was making any sense. Getting answers out of Con was difficult at the best of times. When his emotions were involved, it was damn near impossible.

"Why would Cecily say a thing like that?" she asked. "And come to think of it, why didn't she tell you about the baby?"

Abandoning the scraps, Con took another drag on his cigarette. "I've been asking myself the same thing. She knew I was with the bureau. It wouldn't have been hard to find me. Maybe she didn't want to keep the baby, and my support would have given her less excuse to give him up," he said, the look in his eyes empty.

"Or maybe she was afraid to tell you."

Robbie could understand someone's being afraid of

him. His size alone was pretty intimidating. And this Cecily couldn't have known him very well, couldn't have known about the tender vulnerable man beneath the rock-hard protective shell.

"So what's going to happen?" she asked, wondering about the baby, Con's son. The closest thing she was probably ever going to have to a child of her own—her best friend's son.

"I called social services and they're sending someone out tomorrow afternoon to ask questions and fill out some forms. Then I can meet him."

"And then what?"

Con took another drag on his cigarette. "They'll run blood tests to make certain I'm really his father," he said, his gravelly voice subdued. "Then we go to court."

"Why court?" That didn't sound good. She took a sip of her beer.

"I have to petition for custody and there'll be a hearing. The judge decides whether or not I'm fit to be a parent."

He stared at the glowing tip of his cigarette as if it held some sort of wisdom. Clearly, were he the judge presiding over the case, he'd lose.

Robbie hated it that Con saw so little worth in himself, but then, with the lessons life had taught him growing up, she couldn't blame him. Still, he was a good man with a loving heart if he'd only learn to trust himself enough to believe that.

"I don't know anybody else more fit to be a parent," she said, as sure of that as she was that the sun was going to shine in Phoenix the next day.

"I've never held a baby." There was no emotion in his voice, none apparent in his face. He was all agent, just stating the facts.

"What about Pete and Marie Mitchell's son, Scotty?"

"Marie laid him on my lap once when he was asleep. And she was right there beside me the entire five seconds."

Robbie wasn't about to give up. "So you'll learn how to hold a baby. We can run out to a store and buy a doll that's the right size to practice on. We'll get one that comes with diapers and learn that, too, while we're at it."

She finished her beer and grabbed Con's cigarette for one last puff. She put it out. "Come on, let's go now before they close." All at once she couldn't wait to get started, to make certain they were prepared. He wasn't going to lose his son, certainly not to the same institution that had failed him so miserably.

He didn't budge. "Most of what it takes to be a parent can't be practiced on a doll."

The hollow look in his eyes almost made Robbie forget twenty years of hiding her love for this man. But now, more than ever, he needed her friendship—something that would be lost forever if he knew her real feelings. She was his anchor. Always had been.

And that was far more important than any physical love she might crave.

She looked at him now, resisting the urge to run her fingers through his hair. Buddies didn't touch each other that way. "You're a good man, Con Randolph. You know what's important, what matters in life. And that's all it takes to be a good parent. The rest you learn as you go."

"What matters, Robbie?" He frowned. "I don't have any idea what matters. Not anymore."

She wasn't buying it. "Yes, you do, Con. You just stopped listening to your heart. But it's still in there." She tapped his chest. "And maybe this baby is just what's needed to get you listening again."

He lit another cigarette. "I smoke like a chimney."

"So quit."

"My job's dangerous."

"So's driving a car, breathing the smog, having me for a friend." She grinned at him.

Life was dangerous. He knew that more than most. But he was also doing something to try to make the world a safer place. Who better to be trusted with the life of a youngster than one trained to protect?

He looked over at her, his glance unusually personal. "Having you for a friend has never been dangerous, Robbie. It's the one thing I've done right."

Tears sprang to her eyes and she couldn't hold his gaze. She reached for his cigarette, took a puff and then started to grind it out in the ashtray.

"Hey, don't!" Con said, grabbing the cigarette from her.

"You're trying to quit, too, remember?" she said as she tried to snatch it back.

"Right." With one last puff he put out the cigarette. "Let's go to the store."

Robbie wasn't about to give him a chance to change his mind. She pulled her keys from the pocket of her pants. "We can take my truck," she said.

He immediately grabbed the keys. "I'll drive."

And for once Robbie let him. Her mind was elsewhere.

A baby. Con's flesh and blood. A child I didn't even know existed an hour ago, and yet I feel like I already know him. I'll be an auntie. I can take him to the newsroom, maybe even on a job or two when he gets older. We can take him to the zoo, teach him to swim....

"Hey, Robbie, you doing anything tomorrow afternoon?" Con asked as he locked his front door behind them.

She was pretty certain she had an interview with the governor. "Nope."

"You wanna be here when the social worker comes?"

"Sure." She wanted it more than anything else she'd ever wanted, except maybe for Con to love her the way she loved him.

They climbed into her truck. "I want you to meet him, Robbie."

Already half in love with this child she'd never met simply because he was Con's, Robbie's heavy heart lightened just a little. "Good." *A baby. We're gonna have a baby....*

ROBBIE PULLED UP in front of Con's house the next afternoon with a stomach full of butterflies. She'd wanted a baby of her own to love ever since she could remember, and now at thirty-three, with no one even calling her for a date, playing auntie to Con's son was probably as close as she was ever going to get.

Climbing out of her truck, she smoothed her hands down her favorite cotton top, making sure it was still tucked into the matching cotton shorts she'd hardly ever worn. She could do this.

Con was in the kitchen when she let herself in, leaning over the breakfast bar. She'd left him in the exact same position the evening before.

"You been at that all night?" she teased, trying to see around him to the plastic toy on the counter.

"Lay off, Robbie. I just want to be ready in case the woman from social services puts me to the test."

Robbie came around the bar and climbed onto a stool so she could judge his progress. "She's not bringing the baby with her."

"It doesn't hurt to be prepared."

He held the tiny plastic feet between his thumb and

forefinger, raising the doll just enough to slide the diaper beneath its bottom. She was impressed. The night before he'd stood the baby on its head trying the exact same maneuver.

"If only Pete Mitchell could see you now," she said, grinning.

"Shut up, Robbie."

Con looked so right, tending to the make-believe baby. This huge rugged man diapering a child's toy.

As soon as he'd finished, she took the doll, inspecting his work, holding on to her composure by a thread. "You've improved."

He grabbed the doll back by the hair on its head, ripping off the diaper and starting the process again, concentrated intent in every move.

Robbie grinned. "We'll have to work on the rest of your handling there, Randolph," she said just as the doorbell rang.

Her heart leaped. Were they ready?

Con shoved the doll in the oven.

It was only as they were walking together to the front door that Robbie noticed the absence of a cigarette in Con's vicinity. There were no ashtrays around, either.

SOCIAL SERVICES HAD SENT Sandra Muldoon again. Par for the course, Con thought, that the state had seen fit to send the same uptight woman to his door after he'd spent half the night hoping for a more amenable sort.

"So you see, Mr. Randolph," she was saying, "you're asking the impossible if you hope to convince the court that the child would be better off with a man in your position than with a normal loving family."

Con's blood burned at the woman's words, even as his doubts grew. By what right *did* he think he deserved to disrupt the child's life? Especially when he knew he couldn't hope to provide for him the way a married couple could. He needed a cigarette.

"I would think the state would have its work cut out trying to convince the court why a son should *not* be with his biological father," Robbie jumped in. "Especially when that father is not only law-abiding, but law-enforcing. A man who's given his life to making the world a safer place for his son to grow up. And one who, I might add, is financially more than capable to provide for a child," Robbie finished, glaring at the woman.

As much as he appreciated her spirited defense, Con hated being talked about as if he wasn't there. And he preferred to fight his own battles.

"I'm sure we all recognize the importance of Mr. Randolph's job," Sandra Muldoon said. "But that doesn't take away the threat of danger his job poses to the child. And a child needs far more than financial support.'' Her tone continued to be as prudish as it had been the day before.

"You're talking about love, ma'am," Robbie said, leaning closer to the woman, "and how can you possibly measure the love a father has for his son?"

"What's his name?" Con blurted out. He didn't do love. And he still needed a cigarette.

"His mother called him Joey." The woman's lips pursed disapprovingly. "His adoptive family will probably rename him when he goes to live with them."

"Rename him?" Con was taken aback. "We're talking about my son here, not a possession. You don't rename people."

"Nonetheless an adoptive family has the right to change the child's name. In the case of babies, most do."

"I like 'Joey,'" Con said.

She ignored that. "I've set up an appointment for the baby to have a blood test tomorrow morning. I suggest you do the same for yourself."

"Fine."

She slipped her papers back into the folder. "That's it, then."

"When can I see him?"

"You must understand, Mr. Randolph, things don't look very promising for you. The boy's mother swears you abandoned him. If she hadn't put your name on his birth certificate, we wouldn't have contacted you at all. You're a bachelor, and I gather, from what you and Ms. Blair have told me, you're not dating anyone seriously. You don't even have a mother you can turn to. And your way of life is in no way conducive to raising a child. There doesn't seem to be much point in dragging this out any further. For anyone.''

Con's jaw tightened as he struggled for control. ''When can I see him?'' he repeated, enunciating each word.

The woman stood, her ever-present manila folder clutched to her chest. ''I would at least suggest waiting until after the blood work comes back. There's no point in upsetting the child's schedule until we know for sure.''

Robbie stood, too, ready to do battle. Con read the determination in her eyes.

''It's okay, Robbie,'' he said, moving to stand beside her. ''I disagree,'' he told the social worker. ''There's every point. Since the United States government trusts me with their highest security clearance, I think your court can find me worthy of a visit to my son.''

''But—''

''You've questioned me, seen my home. Now I want to meet my son.''

''Very well.'' Sandra Muldoon's face puckered with displeasure. ''I'll check with his foster mother and see when a visit can be arranged.''

"What about right now?" Robbie asked. "We have the rest of the day free, and most babies are up from their naps by late afternoon. Wouldn't this be as good a time as any?"

The social worker frowned. "I don't know what the foster mother's plans are for the day, and we have no right to disrupt her schedule."

Con didn't see it that way. As the boy's father, he had every right. He had a son to meet.

"I was under the impression that arrangements would already have been made, that this initial interview is only a formality preceding the visit."

"In normal cases, yes..."

"So it wouldn't hurt to call her and ask, would it?" Robbie piped up.

"Well, I..."

Robbie grabbed the telephone from the coffee table. "Here, you can use Con's phone and see if she'd mind just a short visit."

"He can't go to her house. For the baby's safety the foster identity is confidential."

"I solve crimes. I don't commit them." Con kept his rising temper in check, a result of years of training. It was a responsibility that came with being a man his size.

"Then you can bring the baby here, or we'll meet you somewhere else," Robbie said hurriedly, glancing at Con. "That won't be a problem. Con just wants

to see his son, Mrs. Muldoon. Surely you can understand that.''

"All right. I'll call, but I still don't think we'll be
able to do it today.''

The woman dialed, hanging up the phone almost
immediately. "The line's busy. I'll try again tomorrow.'' She began to leave.

Con wasn't going to get this close and give up. He
wanted, needed to see the boy.

"Why not wait right here and try again in a few
minutes?'' he asked, stepping between the woman
and his front door.

Before she had a chance to reply, Robbie joined
him. "Can I get you something to drink while you're
waiting? Iced tea, maybe?''

"Just what exactly is your relationship with Mr.
Randolph?'' the social worker asked her, then looked
from one to the other.

"Like Con told you, we're childhood friends,'' she
said.

"Too bad,'' Mrs. Muldoon sniffed. "He'd at least
have a chance of convincing the courts to take him
seriously if he got married.''

Robbie's gaze flew to Con's face, and he couldn't
believe what her eyes were telling him. She'd been
trying to bail him out since the first day they met,
when she was eight and he was ten, but surely even
Robbie wouldn't go as far as to tie herself to a loveless marriage just to help him out. As for

him...marriage? To Robbie? There was no way. She was his best friend. His only friend.

He wasn't even aware that she'd moved away from him until he heard her speaking to Mrs. Muldoon.

"So can I get you that glass of tea?"

Marry Robbie? No way in hell.

CHAPTER THREE

IT WAS GOING to have to be the woman. He'd been watching Randolph's house for more than a month now, and the only person who'd come over was the woman with the short blond hair, and an old saleslady or something, who didn't count. He was kind of disappointed. It wouldn't work unless Randolph really cared about the woman, and the two of them didn't seem close like a guy and girl should be close. They hung out together a lot, but Randolph never touched her or even looked at her as if he *wanted* to touch her.

He would have liked it a lot better if Randolph was getting into her pants.

But she was going to have to do. He couldn't wait any longer. A plan was formulating in his head, occupying the space that was too filled with bitterness to let him sleep nights. Yeah. It was time.

THE SKY WAS A BLUE so vivid it made your eyes water. Sunshine splashed on the rocks in Con's front yard, turning them into nuggets of gold. A day this perfect was meant for good things. Except that practically every day in Phoenix was this beautiful, and bad things happened all the time. And the June temperatures made those golden rocks hot enough to fry eggs.

Con was sitting in his car waiting for Robbie to get off her truck phone and join him. He was sweating like a pig. He probably could have gotten away with something a little less formal than a suit, but he always felt more in control in his standard agent attire. *They'll probably take one whiff of me and call the health department.*

He honked his horn impatiently, then cranked up the air-conditioning, turning the vents so they all faced him. He was tempted to go without Robbie. Except that he was strangely reluctant to leave her behind. After all, it wasn't every day a man met his kid for the first time.

He saw Robbie's head bob and her free hand gesture wildly in the air. She was getting pretty adamant about what she was saying. Con felt a little sorry for the poor bastard on the other end of the line, whoever he was, but only briefly. Why didn't the guy just hurry up and give in to her so they could go?

The Muldoon woman had tried for almost an hour the day before to reach Joey's foster mother, but to no avail. The woman either had the phone off the hook or spent way too much time gabbing to be caring for an infant. Con had extracted a promise from the social worker that she'd keep trying the woman periodically throughout the evening. And true to her word, Sandra Muldoon had called just as he and Robbie were starting in on the pizza they'd ordered to say that he could meet his son this morning.

He honked the horn again, twice this time for good measure. Robbie had parked her truck in its usual place in front of his house, and now she glared at him through the windshield, flashed him the finger and went right on talking.

Thrumming his fingers on the steering wheel, he glanced at his watch and thrummed some more. He'd told Robbie to be here at nine o'clock sharp. Technically she had five more minutes. And then he was leaving. With or without her.

He pulled a cigarette from the fresh pack on his console, lit it and took a long satisfying drag. He'd give her until the end of his cigarette, and then he was leaving. It was 110 degrees outside. His engine was going to overheat if he sat there much longer.

He took another puff, holding the smoke in his lungs until they felt as if they might burst, and then slowly exhaled. The neighborhood was quiet as usual. Rows of white stucco homes with tile roofs, expensively landscaped yards, mostly desert, though there were a few diehards who paid heavily for the water it took each week to keep a patch of green grass.

Con flicked the ashes off his cigarette and took another long drag.

A couple of yards down from him a kid was raking gravel. The boy had been around for a while now, doing odd jobs for anyone who'd pay him, and from what Con could see, he did a pretty good job. The kid had knocked on Con's door several weeks back offering to trim his bushes; but working in his yard was something Con enjoyed, took pride in. Still, he was glad to see the kid had found some customers.

"Sorry. That was Rick," Robbie said, climbing into the car. "He wants me to have another shot at Cameron Blackwell." She was wearing a denim skirt with some pink top he'd never seen before. He hadn't even known she *owned* a skirt.

"When is Hastings going to figure out that Blackwell wants to be left alone?"

She buckled her seat belt and reached for Con's cigarette. "Not as long as Blackwell's living here. Can you just imagine what a coup it would be to get the nation's most talked-about recluse cartoonist to actually give an interview? We'd be picked up by all the wires."

"How you gonna get to him to even ask for an interview?" Con maneuvered his way out of his neighborhood and turned south on Hayden. It was a twenty-minute drive to the social-services office where his son would be waiting for him. Twenty minutes to keep his mind off the upcoming meeting. He wished Robbie hadn't finished the damn cigarette. He'd promised himself it would be his last until after he saw the kid.

She shrugged. "I haven't figured that out yet, but I'll come up with something."

"You've been after him for more than a year."

"So, I'll keep after him for another ten if that's

what it takes. All I want to do is talk to the guy. He's got a lot of fans and has gotten mighty rich because of it. People want to know more about him.''

"They paid for comics. They got comics. Can't they be satisfied with that?"

She reached for his cigarettes, helping herself to one. "Honestly, Con, aren't you the least bit curious about Blackwell?"

He might have been if he wasn't so sympathetic with the cartoonist's desire for privacy. "Nope. And why don't you buy yourself a pack of cigarettes, for God's sake, and leave mine the hell alone?"

She grinned at him. "I can't. I quit."

He grunted, applying the brake as the light up ahead turned yellow. He could wait for the red light. Now that he was finally on his way, he was in no hurry to get there. What if he made the kid cry? Or, God forbid, what if they handed the boy to him? Expected Con to hold him? He couldn't do that. Not in front of them. He'd just have to make sure Robbie was the one they handed him to.

"Did you get downtown for your blood test?" she asked, taking her time about enjoying his cigarette.

"Yeah." He'd been at the forensic lab at six o'clock that morning.

She was oddly quiet as he sailed through green lights at the next couple of intersections. At this rate he'd be there five minutes sooner than he needed to be. Where were red lights when he needed them? Or Robbie's chatter, for that matter?

She continued to puff on his cigarette. He was going to buy her a damn case of them for her birthday. Exhaling, she lifted the cigarette to his lips.

"I'm going to say something here," she began, "and I don't want you to answer or argue. Just listen, OK?"

Con nodded, fortifying himself on nicotine.

She stared at the road in front of them, a frown on her face, and he braced himself. She was powering up for something, but if she thought he was going to move that damn water bed for her one more time, she could think again. He'd told her the last time that she'd better make up her mind once and for all whether or not she wanted to sleep beneath the window or across from it, because he wasn't tearing down the bed again.

"I just want you to know," she said at last, "that if it comes to it, if they really push you about being married, you can say we're engaged."

He almost dropped the cigarette.

"You hungry?" he asked. "I'm driving through for a burger."

"I mean it, Con."

"You hungry?"

She shook her head. "I ate breakfast before I left. So you'll tell them? If you have to?"

Con looked around for a burger joint. He needed something to sink his teeth into. And while he was at it, he kept his eye open for a bank robbery, a shootout, a gang war. Something he knew he could handle.

"Answer me, Con."

"You told me not to."

"Okay, I'm *un*telling you."

"You're crazy." There wasn't a burger joint on this part of Hayden, so why the hell was he looking?

"I knew you'd say that, which is why I told you not to say anything. It's not crazy, Con. According to old sourpuss Muldoon, it may be the only way you can get little Joey."

"He's my son. I'll get him."

"He's a ward of the state, Con. You know how sticky the rules get sometimes."

He wasn't going to think about those years. Not now. "Right. Like they'd believe an engagement without the wedding."

"I don't have a problem with a wedding."

Con swore. Why in hell had he wanted her to come with him? He knew she never shut up. "But you'd sure as hell have a problem with what comes afterward."

"I would not."

"You're crazy," he said again.

Her blue eyes flashed. "I'm perfectly sane, Connor Randolph. And obviously the only one of us here who is. There's a little boy waiting whose whole life could depend on your being married. I'm not involved with anyone. You don't date any women long enough to be involved. We get along OK most of the time. There's no reason we couldn't cohabitate."

"You're outta your mind."

"I'm tired, Con." The depressed tone in her voice grabbed him. Robbie never got depressed, she just got tougher. "I'm tired of putting up with crap from the guys. Tired of being the odd one out all the time. Tired of being alone. I'm thirty-three years old and there's still no knight in shining armor coming around to sweep me off my feet." She paused, took a deep breath. "I want to be a mother, Con. If I marry you, I get Joey, too."

He felt like he was coming unglued. He'd never heard her talk this way before. He had to shut her up. Fast. "You can mother the boy all you want, Robbie, but there's no chance in hell of our getting married."

"Why not, if it's the only way to get Joey?"

"It won't be."

"But what if it is?"

He refused to answer. He should definitely have done this without her.

"What are you afraid of?"

Her words were nothing but challenge. He knew that. And had it been anyone else but Robbie issuing them, he'd have let them go. "Nothing. I'm afraid of nothing." But he knew it wasn't true. He was scared that they weren't going to let him have his son.

"Then what's the problem? You got some hot broad I don't know about?"

He was silent. She knew he didn't.

He always told her about the women he dated, if for no other reason than to allow her common sense to keep him from finding himself making do, getting trapped in a loveless relationship. Because as far as he was concerned, that was the only kind there was.

"Once we're married, the courts would be out of it, Con," she said, talking like it was a done deal. "They wouldn't have any say in how we conduct the marriage. We could carry on just like we are except I'd give up my apartment and rent one of the empty rooms in that big house of yours. I'd probably help with the dishes a little more, and if you're nice, you might even be able to talk me into going to the grocery store for you."

"No," he said flatly. If she thought she was going to bulldoze her way through this one, she was wrong.

"I've thought about this all night, Con. It can work."

"Enough." Marriage with Robbie? No way in hell.

They'd arrived. Con stubbed out his cigarette and pulled into a parking place by the entrance. He'd say one thing for Robbie. She'd certainly managed to distract him from the job at hand.

"Just remember," she said softly, walking beside him to the door of the social-services office. "They give you any flak, you tell them we're engaged."

As they entered the building, Con broke out in a cold sweat.

A BLUE-CARPETED HALLWAY lined with closed doors on either side stretched before them. Most of the doors had white-lettered plastic signs pasted on them, and Robbie strode forward, reading each one they approached. If she left it up to Con, they'd be back in the car. She'd seen the hunted look in his eyes the second he'd stepped into the building.

"Here it is," she said, finding the door marked *playroom.* Karen Smith, the social worker who'd volunteered to supervise this meeting, had thought it best to have Con see the baby in an impersonal atmosphere. So far, the social-services representatives were treating Con like a headache they knew would eventually disappear. If Robbie hadn't been so angry for Con's sake, she'd have felt sorry for them. They didn't have a clue who they were dealing with.

Con stood frozen beside her, so she reached for the doorknob.

"Wait." His jaw was tense, his body tight as if poised for battle. Her heart twisted. How many times had she stood by and watched Con fight for what should have been rightfully his? Fight—and lose. She wasn't going to let him lose this time.

"Putting if off isn't going to make it any easier, Randolph," she said.

Con nodded and opened the door himself.

She saw the baby almost immediately. His carrier seat was in the middle of a small table that was rimmed with an army of empty miniature wooden chairs.

"Ms. Blair? Mr. Randolph? I'm Karen Smith. It's nice to meet you."

Robbie was only vaguely aware of the tall young woman who came forward to shake Con's hand. She couldn't pull her gaze from the baby sleeping just a few feet in front of her. So small. So defenseless.

Con's son.

"Ms. Smith." Con's voice rumbled beside her, as terse as always. No pleasantries there.

She needed to run interference for him, to show some social graces before they blew this altogether, but still she stared at the child, feeling as if she'd been poleaxed. The baby was too precious for words.

She glanced over at Con, wondering if he felt the same strange attachment she felt to the little being, who was completely unconscious of their presence. Con was staring at the baby, too. She'd never seen him look scared before, but she suspected that was just what she was seeing in his tense wide-eyed expression now.

"May I hold him?" Robbie asked the social worker, afraid for Con, afraid for the baby he'd unknowingly given life to. Would either of these two Randolph males have the chance to give each other the love they both deserved?

"Of course." Karen stood aside as Robbie moved toward the sleeping infant.

She slid her hands beneath his little body and lifted him gently into her arms. His warmth, his weight as he settled against her, was immediately soothing.

Nothing had felt so right in her life.

"Oh, my God, Con, he looks like you!" she cried softly, studying the baby's perfect little features, his dimpled chin, his tiny baby nose. She wasn't ever going to be able to let him go. She looked at his father again and had to consciously restrain herself from going over and holding him, too.

Con remained just in front of the closed door, staring at the child in her arms, his eyes smoldering with emotion. He swallowed, once, with an effort.

"Come, Mr. Randolph. Meet Joey," Karen said, reaching for Con's elbow.

He moved away from her, instead, taking a seat in one of the armchairs in the waiting area of the playroom, his gaze never leaving the baby Robbie held. He'd wrapped himself in control.

Robbie could see the doubt in Karen's eyes as she watched Con, could almost hear the negative thoughts whirring through the social worker's mind. But Karen didn't know Con like Robbie did. She had no idea how fiercely Con felt those things that touched him, how difficult it was for him to deal with those feelings. She didn't know, as Robbie did, that Con would give up his life to protect this child he couldn't yet approach.

She walked over to Con, perched on the arm of his chair and willed him to stay put.

"Look at him, Con. He's got your chin."

Con looked. And swallowed again. His hands gripped the arms of the chair as if he was ready to push off. But he didn't. His gaze never left the baby.

Robbie picked up one limp little hand. "Look at his fingernails!" she exclaimed in hushed tones. "They're so tiny." She could hardly believe how perfect this small being was, or how fiercely she felt the need to protect him from whatever life had in store.

"He's got all ten fingers—" she looked down "—and toes."

Con nodded.

"He's perfectly healthy, though he does top the size charts," Karen said, coming over to join them. She sat in the chair across from them, leaning to rest her forearms on her knees. Robbie felt like a fly under a microscope beneath her watchful eye.

"When's his blood work due back?" Con asked abruptly.

"We should have the results sometime next week."

Con nodded again. "I'll have his room ready."

"Slow down there, Mr. Randolph. There's no guarantee you're going to get the child even if it turns out he's yours."

"He's mine." Robbie heard the anger in Con's voice, though she doubted the social worker did. Con had perfected the art of concealing his feelings by the time he was ten. Just as she'd learned to read what he kept hidden. Most of the time.

"It would really be best if you didn't keep telling yourself that. Not until we're certain," Karen said. "And like I said, even if he's yours, there's still no guarantee you'll get him."

Robbie knew Con wouldn't thank her for it, but she couldn't sit quietly by while Karen hurt him. "Joey's his," she said, looking from Con to the baby she held. "You can tell just by looking at them. Joey's got the same dimple in his chin that Con does."

The social worker looked from Con to the baby. "Maybe so, but it's important that you both understand. Being Joey's father in no way means Mr. Randolph will get the child. There are many other things to consider."

"Such as?"

Karen noticed the steel in Con's voice that time. She looked a little less sure of herself as she answered him. "There'll be a thorough background check on you, for one."

Con nodded, undaunted.

"You'll have to be able to prove an ability to support the child."

Con nodded again, holding Karen's gaze unwaveringly.

"And most importantly your lifestyle will be examined. The judge will want to be certain that the life you have to offer this child is the one best suited to him."

Robbie sensed Con's barely perceptible flinch. How she wished there was some way she could take away his pain. As hard as he'd tried, Con had never measured up, not in the eyes of his foster parents, not in the eyes of the school system and most especially, not in his own.

"And quite frankly, Mr. Randolph," Karen continued, garnering confidence again, "from what we've seen so far, I don't think you should count on getting the child. As far as the courts are concerned, you abandoned him. And we have a family, a two-parent family, already approved to adopt him.''

"I did not abandon my son.''

"So you say. That's for the court to determine.'' Karen paused. "And the fact still remains that you do not appear to have much to offer the child. Certainly not when compared to the childless couple whose whole lives will revolve around him.''

"I'm his father. I offer him that.''

"*If* indeed you are his father, you'd be a single father at best. I'm sorry, Mr. Randolph. If you were at least married, maybe you'd have a better chance, but as things stand…''

Here it comes, Robbie thought, her chest tightening. She'd feared that it would. But could she really do it? Could she tie herself to Con knowing he'd never love her the way she loved him? Could she risk his finding out how she really felt?

"There's no law against single parenting.'' Con wasn't backing down. Robbie breathed a small sigh of relief. Maybe they wouldn't need her drastic solution.

"No,'' Karen said. "But statistics do show that a child has more opportunity to prosper in a two-parent home. And that's not the only issue here. You're an FBI agent, Mr. Randolph. Your job is incredibly dangerous. What becomes of Joey if anything happens to you?''

Con was silent and Robbie could tell Karen knew she'd scored. The woman's features relaxed as if her battle was won.

"But even danger aside, you work long hours, odd hours. You're gone for days at a time. Who'd watch your son then?"

"A sitter."

Robbie held Joey closer. The sleeping baby sighed and nestled contently against her breast.

"You're asking the judge to place the child with a sitter, rather than a complete family unit who'll love him, who'll be there for him?" Karen asked.

"He's my son."

Karen sat forward, clutching her hands together, her eyes worried again. Robbie realized that the woman truly cared about little Joey, about his future. "Please try to understand, Mr. Randolph," Karen said. "If indeed Joey is your son, you've got to want what's best for him. That's all the court wants, too."

"A boy needs his father."

"Yes, sir. But he needs a mother, too."

They were going to lose him. Robbie could see the writing on the wall as clearly as if it had been emblazoned there. Suddenly the baby stretched in her arms, opening his innocent blue eyes to frown up at her. *Who are you?* his gaze seemed to ask. But he didn't cry.

"He'll have a mother," Robbie said. There was no more time to think about it. She couldn't let Con lose his son. *She* couldn't lose this precious child.

"He will?" Karen said, glancing from her to Con. "I understood from Sandra Muldoon that you weren't currently involved, Mr. Randolph."

"I'm n—"

"He is with me," Robbie blurted, before Con blew things once and for all. He'd never be able to live with himself if the courts gave his son away. "Con asked me to marry him just this morning." Robbie couldn't believe she was saying the words even as she heard them come out of her mouth. Marriage to Con would be sheer torture, loving him as she did. But she just didn't see any other way. Without a wife, Con wasn't going to get Joey.

She was strong. She'd been loving Con for years without anybody's being the wiser. She could handle this marriage. She was sure she could. Especially with compensation like Joey. She'd be a mother. And half a dream come true was better than none, wasn't it?

Yes, she was positive she could handle it.

Until she glanced over at Con. He was looking at her through the eyes of a stranger. A stranger she'd just committed herself to marry.

"Congratulations," Karen said, smiling for the first time since they'd entered the room.

Joey started to cry.

CHAPTER FOUR

No! CON KNEW he had to stop this craziness. Now.

But how? Karen Smith was right. He had nothing to offer the child. At least nothing of any merit—unless he married Robbie. She was the only good in his life. Always had been.

But he couldn't marry her. He couldn't even *think* about marrying her.

The baby was working himself up into a real squall. Robbie held him higher and started bouncing him.

"Here, let me have him," Karen said, coming over. "He's probably hungry."

Con looked at Robbie, saw the pleading in her eyes, and realized his entire life hinged on this moment. He had to come through—whether he thought he could or not.

"I'll take him," he said, staking his claim, his right to be the one to see to the boy's needs. He reminded himself over and over of the plastic toy he'd practiced on for all those hours. He could do this. He reached for his son.

A slow smile broke out across Robbie's face, and if he didn't know better, he'd think there was a hint of tears in her eyes as she handed the baby to him.

"You've got a ball player there, Randolph," she said, her words as tough as ever.

His kid was a little heavier than the plastic one; squirmy, too, but Con forced himself to concentrate on getting it right. He kept one hand under the baby's head, just like Robbie had shown him the other night, and used his other to support the body. The little boy's face was red and all scrunched up as he howled his displeasure.

"You got a bottle?" he asked Karen as if he'd been doing this all his life. But he was sweating. And shaking, too. His kid sure had a healthy set of lungs.

"His foster mother left one. I'll get it," Karen called, pulling a bottle from the diaper bag on the table beside the baby's carrier seat. "It's still warm." She handed the bottle to Con.

"What kind of formula is he on?" Robbie asked, raising her voice to be heard over the baby's crying.

Con took the bottle. Formula. Right. He remembered Marie Mitchell talking about that once.

"He's on soy milk," Karen said, taking her seat across from them. "He was pretty colicky there for a while, but the soy milk seems to have helped."

Con looked at the wailing baby in his arms. The kid's face was still all screwed up and red, but suddenly, out of nowhere, Con felt like grinning. He was doing it. He was holding his son.

"You might want to give him that bottle." Robbie said, leaning over to try to guide the nipple into Joey's tiny mouth.

"Wait for it to cool," Con said, jerking the bottle back. Warm milk was disgusting. He wasn't going to force it on his kid.

The baby continued to cry, though he quieted for a moment when Con started to bounce him gently.

"It's supposed to be warm, Randolph," Robbie said, smiling. "He'll get stomach cramps if it's not warm. Now feed the poor thing."

She reached over again, guiding the bottle to the baby's mouth. Con just held on.

The baby latched on to the nipple, pulling it into his mouth with a strength that amazed Con, and the room was instantly silent except for the loud sounds of Joey's sucking. The kid had an appetite. Almost as if he'd stepped outside himself, Con saw what was happening. Saw and was filled with the strangest conglomeration of feelings.

He was feeding his son.

"WE CAN'T GET MARRIED." Con sat at his breakfast bar, smoking a cigarette, a cold beer on the counter in front of him. They'd been at it for more than an hour, ever since they'd returned from downtown.

"We're getting married, Con. Get over it." He'd given Robbie her own pack of cigarettes, but she was sharing his, anyway. What was it with the woman? Did she really think it made a difference to her lungs whose cigarettes she smoked?

"It'll never work."

"It has to work."

"Just because you think something is best doesn't make it so."

"It does if I refuse to believe anything else. Joey needs us, Con. Can you honestly sit there and tell me you're going to let him down?"

Here we go again. They'd been traveling in circles and Con was getting nowhere but dizzy. She was leaving him no choice—he had to be blunt.

"You're my only real friend, Rob."

"And you're mine." Her eyes went soft on him.

He hated it when they did that.

"What better basis for a partnership?" she asked.

"And how long do think we'd stay friends?" he shot back.

Robbie shrugged, fiddling with her cigarette in the ashtray between them. "I guess that depends on us, doesn't it?" She looked up at him with her "I mean business" look.

Con sighed. He was in for a long day.

"We can do this, Con. It's because we're such good friends that it *will* work. We understand each other. We're going into this with our eyes open. Neither of us has false expectations."

Con didn't come up with an immediate counterargument, and that bothered him. He wasn't going to let her talk him into this. He couldn't marry her.

"This is a big house, friend," she said. "I think we can manage to share it without killing each other."

Sharing the house with her wasn't the problem. Marriage was. "For how long?"

She blinked. "I don't know. I hadn't thought about it. As long as it takes, I guess."

He pinned her with a relentless stare. "What? A year? Two, maybe?"

"Is that what you want?"

"I don't want. Period."

"If it would make you feel better, we can put a time limit on it, but I think it might work better if we just say we'll stay together until one of us isn't satisfied anymore."

Again Con didn't have an immediate counterargument, only a gut feeling that this was all wrong. They smoked silently for a couple of minutes. Both of them regrouping, he was afraid.

"Why?" he suddenly blurted, finding that he had to know.

"Why what?"

"Why are you doing this? You've always had dreams of your big white wedding, your knight in shining armor. Why ruin that by tying yourself to me?"

"My knight stood me up."

Her mouth smiled, but her eyes didn't. He wished he hadn't asked.

"He could be waiting on your doorstep tomorrow," he told her awkwardly, rusty in the platitude department.

She shook her head. "I'm not the type of woman

a knight rescues, Con. He wants someone soft and feminine. Someone who needs rescuing, makes him feel like a man. Someone who wears makeup.''

Con took a long swig of beer. He was getting in way over his head. ''You don't want me, Robbie.''

''I want to help you. I want to be Joey's mother.'' She looked up at him. ''And I want a wedding ring. I want the guys at work—and their wives—off my back. I want to be invited to parties again, parties that you have to be part of a couple to attend. I want someone around to help me move the TV when I'm tired of where it is.''

''You never said you were having troubles at work.''

''I'm not. Not really. You can't blame the guys, Con. Their wives just don't like it that they hang out with a woman all the time. A single woman.''

He still couldn't marry her.

''What about sex?''

She blushed, looked away. She didn't say a word. Con had never seen Robbie speechless. He might have enjoyed the moment if he wasn't hating it so much.

''I'm a man, not a monk.'' He pushed his advantage.

''I know that.'' She still wasn't looking at him.

''We can't get married, Robbie.''

She lit another cigarette, watching the tip of it glow. ''Could you be discreet?''

''What?''

"When you have your women, couldn't you be discreet? You know, make sure no one I knew ever heard about it?"

"This is asinine." He was talking about his sex life with Robbie. They'd talked about everything else in their lives, but they never ever talked about sex. Now he knew why.

He took another swig of beer.

"Okay." She gave him an awkward grin, obviously finding the conversation as embarrassing as he did. "I'll be discreet, too."

Con almost choked on his beer. *She'd* be discreet? She was planning to sleep with other men while she was married to him?

And then another thought occurred to him. Robbie had sex? He felt pretty damn foolish, but he'd never seen her in that light. He hadn't pictured her as virginal, exactly, he just hadn't pictured her that way at all.

"So when you think we should do it?" she asked.

Do it? She wanted to have sex with him? Robbie and him?

"How about July third?" she continued. "That would give me two weeks to arrange enough of a wedding to convince Karen Smith we're legit. And I have that long weekend off over the Fourth so we could use those days to get me moved in before I have to be back at work."

The wedding. She was back to the damn wedding.

Not sex. Which was just as well. He couldn't even think about Robbie and—

"What about your parents?" he asked, suddenly figuring out how he was going to talk her out of this craziness. They'd never in a million years convince her parents that he and Robbie had suddenly fallen in love.

"They'll be there of course. It would kill them if we got married without them."

"It would kill them to hear what you're suggesting."

Con could just imagine her father's reaction when he heard that Robbie wanted to marry him. Phoenix Police Captain Stan Blair knew what a messed-up kid Con had been, knew how little he really had to offer. Which was why Con had never given the man any reason to worry about him and his daughter. Con had always been welcome in their home, which meant more to Con than anyone would ever know, and he didn't want to lose that.

Robbie laughed at him. "Sometimes you're so obtuse, Randolph. Mom'll be ecstatic. She's always hoped we'd get married. And Dad'll just be glad to know we're finally getting on with it."

The nicotine must have gone to her head. "You're crazy, Rob. Lying won't work with me and you know it. You tell your dad you're marrying me and he'll be at my door with his gun pulled."

"He retired from the force last year, Con, you know that. He doesn't carry a gun anymore."

"They aren't going to like it, Robbie."

"You leave them up to me. Trust me. It'll be fine. Now is July third OK for you?"

Con had no idea whether July third was OK for him. He couldn't consider this. He just couldn't.

"They'd have to know the truth," he said.

"No! No one's going to know." She was sounding her bossiest. "In the first place, the truth *would* bother them, and in the second place, social services is going to be questioning everyone before they give Joey to us. We can't take any chances."

God. The woman had an answer for everything. Every damn thing. Except one. He couldn't marry her.

"You going to let them take Joey, Con? You going to let them give him away?"

"No." That was the one thing he was absolutely sure of. The boy was his. He was going to raise him.

"Then clear your calendar for July third. And next time Karen Smith calls, invite her to the wedding."

STAN AND SUSAN Blair lived in Sedona. They'd moved to the small Arizona artists' community shortly after Stan's retirement from the Phoenix police force. Robbie had missed having her parents close by at first, but she always enjoyed the two-hour drive to Sedona. Or she had until this time.

This Sunday, the barren desert land that stretched for miles and miles between Phoenix and Sedona failed to occupy her imagination. Instead of the pioneer gold miners and Indian families who'd once traipsed across the unforgiving land, all she could think about was the news she had for her parents. And the cigarette she wanted.

She was going to marry Con. Oh, he hadn't agreed yet. But he would. Because of Joey. Her parents would be delighted of course. She hadn't been lying when she'd assured Con of that. But only if they believed she and Con were in love. Which was why she was making this trip alone. Con would have insisted on coming along if he'd known what she was up to. He'd never have left her to face her parents alone, especially when he really expected the scene to be ugly.

But it was going to be hard enough to reveal her love for Con to her parents. She didn't want to do it in front of him. She wanted him as far away as humanly possible. Because while he'd see her act loving in the coming weeks for Joey's sake, he'd think it was only that—an act. But today, while she was convincing her parents, there would be no pretending.

She was actually going to marry Con. There were times in the past few days when she'd had to pull herself right down out of the clouds at the thought. Marriage to Con was what she'd wanted more than anything else since the first stages of puberty had hit her.

But not like this. Never like this. Yes, she would wear his ring. Have his name. Share his home. But not his bed. Instead, she'd be home alone in his house when he went to other women's beds. And she'd have to pretend that she didn't care what he'd done when he came home.

And she'd do it because she couldn't face the alternative. She couldn't offer herself to Con and have him turn her down. It wasn't his fault she wasn't attractive to men. She was too aggressive, too bossy. She didn't wear the right clothes, didn't laugh at the right things. She didn't giggle at all. And she liked being on top.

His friendship was one of the most important things in her life; he brought her more happiness than anyone else ever had. And she'd lose it all if she was ever stupid enough to ask him for something he couldn't give her, if she tried to give him something he didn't want.

If she'd had her choice, she'd rather never marry Con than marry him under these circumstances. She wasn't a complete fool. She knew she was letting herself in for a load of hurt. But what choice did she have? She couldn't let him lose Joey. *She* couldn't lose Joey. Sure, Con had said she could mother the baby without marrying him. But that might prove difficult when Joey belonged to another family.

Besides, as much as the marriage would hurt at times, it would help, too. Not only would she feel comfortable in the social circle at work, but she'd never again lie in bed at night, knowing that if she got sick, or heard a strange noise, there'd be no one around to call out to.

Life was good.

Her parents owned a condo that backed on the foothills of the breathtaking Red Rock Mountains. Pulling into the driveway, Robbie thought how lucky her parents were to have been able to retire in such a gorgeous area.

Little Joey would be lucky, too, coming here for visits during his growing-up years—

Robbie froze, her hand still on her keys as the ramifications of what she was doing really hit home. She was not only going to be Con's wife, she was going to be a mother. Excitement ran through her, giving her goose bumps. Only to be chased away by a surge of panic.

In a few short weeks, if all went well, she was going to have a child to raise. She'd often imagined herself as a mother, had woven wonderful dreams of how it would be. But this wasn't pretense or make-believe. She and Con were going to be *parents*. With another life to consider, to care for, every moment of every day.

And she was not only about to tell her parents she was going to be married, she'd be telling them they were going to be grandparents. She rested her forehead on the steering wheel as the enormity of what she'd set in motion finally sank in. Could she do it? Could she change so many lives simply because, to her, it seemed the only way?

"You OK, girl?"

Robbie jumped as her father opened the door of her truck and peered in, his weathered brow creased.

"Fine, Pop. Just getting up the guts to tell you something." She'd always been straight with her father, just as he'd always been with her.

"Best way is just to say it, girl," he said, leaning both hands on the edge of the door and continuing to watch her. "But it might be good to come on in out of the heat. Let your mother get you a glass of iced tea. Is this something she can hear, too?"

"Yep. And you're right. Let's go get it over with. What's Mom doing?"

"Sitting on the porch with her sewing. Making some fancy tablecloth or something."

He held the door for Robbie as she grabbed her fanny pack and climbed out of the truck.

"You're not sick or anything, are you?" he asked, taking a closer look.

She'd done what she could with her hair and put on her best tank top with a pair of khaki shorts, but she'd had a couple of sleepless nights. She knew she didn't look her best. "No, Pop. I'm not sick. Let's go find Mom."

She followed her father through the cool tiled house to the enclosed air-conditioned porch in back. Robbie had loved the room from the first. It had a great view, and now she looked out over the expanse of land, hoping to catch a glimpse of a coyote or roadrunner or even a family of quail. Anything to avoid her mother's knowing eyes for one last second.

Susan Blair jumped up, dropping her stitchery in a pile on the couch behind her. "Robbie, dear! You're early." She gave her daughter a kiss on the cheek and a hug before stepping back to examine her.

"You look tired, Robbie. You haven't been getting enough sleep, I bet. What's wrong?"

It never changed. Susan's self-appointed role in life was to look after her husband and only child, and while the attention had sometimes felt suffocating during her teenage years, Robbie adored her mother. She adored both her parents. Always had. Maybe because she'd always had Con's to compare them to.

"Mom. Pop, come sit down."

They sat. Her mother beside her on the couch, her father in his recliner across from them. But he didn't recline. He sat forward, his elbows resting on the arms of the chair.

"What is it, girl?" he asked. They both looked at her, worry lining their faces.

"Con and I are getting married."

Shock held them immobile. They stared at her as if waiting for more. She didn't know what else to tell them.

The few seconds of silence that met her announcement seemed interminable. Robbie was sure they could see straight into her heart, that they knew Con didn't love her, couldn't possibly ever love her. How had she ever thought people, especially her parents, would actually believe this charade?

"Well, it's about damn time," Stan said finally as a slow grin spread across his sun-lined face.

"Married, Robbie? You're getting married? To Con?" Her mother's voice broke and suddenly she was laughing and crying at once, pulling Robbie into her arms. And then sitting back to search her daughter's face once again. "You love him, don't you, Robbie, love him with all your heart?"

"I do," Robbie said, feeling like crying herself as she finally admitted aloud what she'd known most of her life.

"When's the wedding?"

"Where's Con?"

"Where will it be?"

"Why isn't he here with you?"

Her parents clamored to know everything. Robbie laughed and answered them as best she could.

"The wedding's July third and Con's working today. But I didn't want to wait any longer to tell you…"

They continued talking about the wedding until lunchtime. Susan had a lot of suggestions, as Robbie had known she would, and she gladly turned over the many details to her mother's capable hands. With only two weeks to plan the wedding, the ceremony would have to be very basic, but with any luck it would be enough to convince social services.

She just wasn't sure Con would agree to the white wedding her mother was insisting on.

As they finished their enchilada feast Robbie said,

"There's something else I need to tell you." She'd put it off as long as she could.

Both of her parents looked up expectantly.

"Con has a son."

"He has a what?"

"Who?"

"Con has a son," Robbie replied. "He's six months old and his name's Joey."

"Why didn't he tell us?" Susan asked, obviously hurt.

"He didn't know himself until a week ago." She wasn't sure how her parents were going to react to this part, but there was no way to hide the truth from them. They loved Con. They'd understand, just as she had. And take little Joey into their hearts.

"Remember that case of his I told you about a year ago last March?"

"The one where the woman was killed," Stan said, nodding.

Robbie proceeded to tell them, in a little less detail than she'd heard it, about the circumstances leading up to Joey's conception and subsequent appearance in Con's life.

"The poor little dear," Susan said when at last Robbie fell silent. "Have you met his foster mother? Is she taking good care of him?"

"We haven't met her, no. But I think she's looking after him just fine. He was clean, well fed..."

They all knew that Joey was probably getting the

finest of care, but still, it couldn't be enough. Not nearly enough.

"I can't imagine Con took it well, having the child in foster care," Stan said.

Robbie thought of the stupor she'd found Con in last week—one that had nothing to do with alcohol.

"No. But you know Con. He'd holding it all inside. Though he's making sure no time is wasted until he has custody."

"When will you get the child?" Susan asked, her eyes full of warm concern—and a bit of grandmotherly anticipation.

Robbie shrugged. "There's a lot of red tape to get through. Sometime in July, we're hoping," she said. There was no reason to worry her parents with the battle that still awaited them regarding Joey's guardianship. She and Con were going to get the baby. There was no other alternative.

ROBBIE'S FATHER followed her back out to the porch after Susan shooed them away from the lunch dishes.

"You sure you're happy, girl? You aren't just doing this for Con's sake?"

Robbie plopped down on the couch and nodded. "I'm sure. I love him, Pop. I always have."

"It's going to be different being his wife. You know that, don't you?"

Robbie blushed. Was her father fixing to give her "the talk" at the tender age of thirty-three? "Mom told me about the birds and the bees when I was ten, Pop,'' she said, grinning at him.

"You need a light?'' he asked, grabbing his lighter off the table.

Robbie shook her head. "I quit.''

"Good for you!'' Stan reached for his pipe, his alternative to the three packs of cigarettes a day he used to smoke, packed it and lit up.

"I need to say this, Robbie.'' He paused, looking more at his pipe than at her. "I raised you to be like me, to have the courage and the conviction to know your own mind and to stand by it, but sometimes I wonder if maybe I did too good a job.''

Robbie frowned. "I don't understand.''

"Con's going to want a *woman* in his bed, Robbie. Not one of the guys.''

They'd always been straight with each other. But it had never hurt like this before.

"You don't think I'm a woman, Pop?''

"Of course I do. You're one hell of a woman. But you're a lot like your old man, too. I'm just saying that maybe you should tone down a bit now that you're getting married. You'll have a man to stick up for you now.''

"You want me to change who I am?''

"Don't get me wrong, honey. I love who you are. I'm proud as hell of what you've become. I just want to see this marriage work.''

"So all that stuff you told me about being my own person, about not being afraid to be who I am—even if that's different—about fighting for what I feel is right, about speaking my own mind—all that was just until I found myself a man to take care of me?" She couldn't believe this was her father talking.

"I want you to be happy, Robbie," he said, his eyes glistening.

Even her own father knew she didn't have what it took to attract and keep a man. But she'd been who she was for thirty-three years. She couldn't change that now. Not for anyone. Not even for Con.

"I'm happy, Pop," she said. But she wasn't sure either one of them believed that.

CHAPTER FIVE

HE NEEDED A CRIB. The baby had to have a place to sleep. Diapers, too. Joey probably wouldn't come with them, like the doll had.

Con sat at his breakfast bar Tuesday night after work making a list. He hadn't seen Robbie since Friday. Hadn't heard from her all weekend. Not that either of them were in the habit of checking in with each other, but they hadn't gone this many days without talking since he'd returned to Phoenix after his stint at the FBI academy in Quantico, Virginia.

Damn. He was probably going to need a load of stuff. Bottles, something to go in them, clothes. He added all that to the list. Was regular soap OK for babies? And he'd need something disposable to wipe Joey off with, too. The doll had come with a little cloth, but he sure as hell wasn't going to be using anything he'd have to clean afterward, and paper towels were probably a little rough. But maybe they'd do at first, if he wet them down. He put disposable cloths down, anyway, just in case he happened to run across some.

He hadn't heard a word from social services since

Friday. If he had, he'd have had a reason to call Robbie.

He wasn't kidding himself. He knew why she hadn't shown up on his doorstep all weekend. The marriage thing. It was already messing things up.

Con looked over his list again, sure he was missing stuff. He wasn't a stupid man. He just had no experience with babies or their needs. So how in hell did he think he could raise one by himself?

He could learn. But was that fair to the boy? When Robbie was so willing to be there to help the two of them muddle through? But was it fair to Robbie to allow her to sacrifice so much?

He picked up his list. Where did one go to get a crib? Back to the store where they'd bought the doll? Or was there a baby store that would have everything he needed? Was there more than one kind of crib? Were some better than others?

And what about a stroller? He sure saw enough of those around. Everyone with a little kid seemed to have one. He added a stroller to his list.

He needed Robbie.

In the past he'd have picked up the phone and called her. Told her to get her ass over here and show him what to do.

But that was then and this was now. Now Robbie thought they should get married. Shopping for stuff with a friend was one thing. Picking out cribs with his potential wife was something else entirely. And way too intimate for him and Robbie.

They weren't even married and he was losing her.

He thought about calling Pete's wife, Marie. She'd know everything he needed, as well as the best place to shop. And Pete could probably give him a few pointers, too. But they weren't too happy with him these days. Not that they'd ever really seen things his way, but once upon a time he'd saved their lives and they'd been grateful. Of course, that was only after he'd put Marie at risk in the first place, believing she'd been involved in some pretty nasty international sabotage.

And ever since that deal with Ramirez went sour a year ago last April, ever since it became public knowledge that an innocent woman had died, Con had been avoiding Pete and Marie Mitchell. Pete had tried to warn Con, way back when they'd been partners on Marie's case, that he was losing it; and he accused Con of going after his man at any cost. Con didn't need to see the condemnation in their eyes to know that Pete had been right. He hated himself enough without that.

What the hell. As long as he was hating himself already...

He lit a cigarette, picked up the phone and called Robbie.

"OK, WE'LL GET MARRIED," he said as soon as she answered.

"Con? Glad to see you've come to your senses. I already told Mom and Pop."

The cigarette shook in his fingers. He wished she hadn't done that. No matter what Robbie said, he knew her parents couldn't have been happy about her announcement. He stood to lose everything in this marriage. Everything but his son.

"You couldn't wait to let me speak to your father?" he said a little more sharply than he intended.

"When would that have been, Con? When Joey was twenty-one? We have a wedding to plan, and if you're going to bring your son home anytime soon, we did need to do it now."

"Plan? What's to plan? We go to the justice of the peace, say a few words and it's done."

"I'm not cheating my parents out of a wedding, Con. Besides, if we want everybody to believe this is the real thing, we have to do it right."

"Meaning?"

"You're going to have to wear a tux."

Hell. He took another puff on his cigarette. The tuxedo wasn't a problem. The wedding was. He couldn't believe Robbie was willing to go through all this for him and Joey. He couldn't believe he'd actually let her.

"Fine."

"Fine?"

"Yes, fine. Now get your ass over here. I need some help getting ready for the kid."

"How do you know I'm not busy?"

"Are you?"

"No."

"You're pushing me, Robbie."

"You're pushing *me*, Randolph. You quit smoking yet?"

He looked at the cigarette burning in the ashtray, wishing he could tell her that at least he'd done that much right.

"No."

"Good. I'm on my way."

HE NEEDN'T have worried. Robbie was as much a pain in the ass as ever. But she took care of the whole shebang. He followed her from store to store, observing and handing over his credit card. It was all relatively simple. Robbie argued with him about everything. Apparently he was a Neanderthal when it came to decorating. He just wanted stuff that worked. She wanted it all to match. He approved of the race-car pattern she picked out for the nursery, as she called the room where the boy would be sleeping, but he gave her a hard time about it, anyway. He liked matching wits with Robbie, always had.

They went for a beer afterward, smoking half a pack of cigarettes. Con was between cases at work and didn't have much to say, but Robbie filled him in on her plans to approach the cartoonist Cameron Blackwell, bouncing ideas off him. And by the time she drove away that night, he'd almost convinced himself that things were back to normal.

Sex hadn't been mentioned all evening. Not once.

THE BLOOD WORK came back inconclusive. There was a seventy percent chance that Con was Joey's biological father.

"What the hell is a seventy percent chance?" Con asked Karen Smith the morning she called to report the results.

"It means you *could* be Joey's father, but it's not enough to prove it. We look for a ninety-eight percent or better to determine conclusive paternity."

"So now what?"

"I'm going to ask you again to reconsider your position, Mr. Randolph," Karen said, speaking to him as his high-school teachers used to when they wanted him to admit to doing something he hadn't done. "If you would only sign the papers, Joey would be out of foster care by the end of the week and into his new home."

"You have a home ready for him?"

"We have prospective parents chosen. They won't be told they have a baby until it's official."

"By official you mean my signature."

"Yes, sir."

"Then why will my signature not gain *me* access to the boy?"

"We've been through all this before, Mr. Randolph," Karen said wearily. "Won't you please reconsider and sign the papers? Let Joey begin his new life?"

For a split second Con considered doing as she asked. He could return all the baby things filling one of his spare rooms upstairs. Get back to his life. Let Robbie get back to hers. Smoke to his heart's content.

But could he send his son the same messages his biological parents had sent him? *We didn't want you.* Could he risk the chance that someone might raise his son to the tune he'd always heard? *You owe us.* Or how about his favorite? *You're a major disappointment.*

"I will not abandon my son."

"You may not have any choice."

"Let's leave that up to the judge," Con said. He wasn't about to get into it with a state employee. Especially one he might need on his side. "What happens next?"

"We'll need more blood work—a DNA screening this time. If you're the boy's father, the DNA will show a more conclusive match."

"Fine."

"Assuming you are the father, we'll also need to send someone back out to your home to see what kind of setup you have there for the baby." She paused. "You do know you'll need to provide a crib and personal things for Joey, don't you?"

"Done."

"He'll need clothes, bottles, blankets, lotions, toys—"

"Done."

"All of it? What about a baby thermometer?"

"That, too." Con jotted it down on a piece of paper. If he didn't have one yet, he would before the day was through. "Come see for yourself."

"You can be sure we will, Mr. Randolph, probably early next week."

He was getting married next week.

"Fine."

"Well, then, if that's all…"

It wasn't all. Not by a long shot. "How soon before we hear back on the DNA?"

"It's hard to say, Mr. Randolph. Sometimes it takes weeks. Of course," she added, softening, "with your connections, you could probably get the lab-work results a lot faster than the state will."

"Consider it done." He told her where to send the baby's blood sample.

"OK, well, after the blood work comes back and all the social workers' reports are turned in, a date will be set for you to appear before the judge. He'll make his determination at that time."

"And I pick up Joey there?"

"*If* you get him. And *if* he's there. It's more likely you'd be instructed to pick him up from his foster home. I'm sure his foster mother will have instructions. In the meantime," she continued, her tone softening again, "you can rest assured he's being very well cared for."

"I want to see him."

"Yes, I rather thought you might. Tell me, Mr. Randolph, when are you and Ms. Blair getting married?"

"Next Wednesday. Robbie's sending you an invitation."

"Oh!" she sounded impressed, pleased. "I mean, I didn't expect it to be so soon. Are you going away for a honeymoon?"

Honeymoon. There wasn't going to *be* any honeymoon in this marriage. "Not until after we have the boy."

"So you'll be home over the Fourth of July weekend?"

"Yes."

"Do you think your people could have the DNA results to us by then?"

"They'll have it as soon as humanly possible once they get the sample."

"Oh. Good," she said, drawing out the *good.* "The thing is, Mr. Randolph, Joey's foster parents have made plans to take their children to Disneyland over the holiday weekend. They'd expected Joey to be with his adoptive parents by then, and they've already made all their reservations. I'm meeting with the judge this afternoon to make other arrangements for Joey that weekend."

Anger burned his gut. His son was in the way. Why in hell was she telling him this when he was helpless to do a damn thing about it? "So?"

"Well, in view of the situation and since you say you're already prepared—and of course because you're going to be married by then—I thought maybe

I'd suggest to the judge that, if the DNA comes back positive, Joey be released to you for that weekend.''

Something that was wound tight inside him relaxed. He was being given a chance. "I'd like that," he said, warning himself not to count on too much. They were letting him baby-sit. That was all. "I'd like that very much.''

"HERE, SPRAY THE HOUSE." Robbie handed Con a can of disinfectant. He was hovering. She couldn't scrub toilets with him hovering. And they only had an hour before Karen Smith arrived for her inspection. It was Monday, the day before Con's cleaning lady was due. And two days before their wedding.

"You spray. I'll clean my own bathrooms."

Robbie laughed. "Have you ever cleaned a bathroom, Connor Randolph?''

"Don't call me that. My foster mother used to call me that. And yes, Miss Priss, I have." He grabbed the cleaning powder, sponge and toilet brush from her arms and handed her the can of disinfectant.

"Make sure you spray the kitchen. I smoke too much in there," he said.

"You smoke too much everywhere."

Her wedding was only forty-eight hours away, and Robbie could almost convince herself she was going to be a real wife as she sprayed the house, doing her best to kill the stale cigarette-smoke odor that permeated everything Con owned. Karen Smith's visit was twofold. She was coming to inspect the nursery and to bring little Joey for Con's second supervised visit with him. The DNA work had not been done yet, since Joey's foster mother had been remiss in getting Joey in for the second blood test. So they couldn't have him to themselves, but at least they were going to get to see him.

There were moments over the past week, dangerous moments, when Robbie had almost let herself believe that her dreams were coming true. In two days she was going to be Con's wife, the mother of his child. She looked around the unusually spotless kitchen and pictured herself there in the early hours of the morning, wearing nothing but a robe she'd pulled on hastily when she'd had to leave Con's bed because their baby had cried. She was heating a bottle of soy milk for Joey and thinking about the glorious hours she'd just spent in Con's arms....

"That should be it," Con said, coming up behind her with his cleaning supplies.

She jumped guiltily, her heart pounding, afraid he'd know what she'd been thinking. Stooping down to hide the flush she could feel rising up her throat and into her cheeks, she swiped at the baseboard.

"Did you get the safety corners on the tables in the living room?" she blurted.

"Done."

"How about the trash?" She berated herself for being a fool. She was going to have more out of life than she'd ever dared hope, and if she allowed her stupid hormones to blow her friendship with Con, she'd never forgive herself.

"Emptied." He put the supplies on a shelf in the laundry room. He was wearing jean shorts and a polo shirt today, looking far more casual than she was used to. His long muscled legs seemed to go on forever.

"You taking the whole day off?" she asked.

"The whole week. I'm between cases."

"Good, you need a break."

"I do not need a break."

Robbie knew better than to argue with that tone. "Whatever," she said.

He reached into the drawer for his pack of cigarettes. "Not now, Randolph," she admonished him. He was the one who'd forbidden smoking in the house at all that day.

He nodded, but when he began pacing like a caged animal, instead, Robbie almost wished she'd let him have his cigarette. He moved about the house, inspecting every spotless room, stopping to look out the living-room window and then beginning his tour again.

She didn't know who was more relieved when the doorbell finally rang.

Con took the baby's carrier from Karen before he even let her in the door. He carried his son into the living room and set him carefully down on the newly polished coffee table. Joey was sleeping.

"Why does he sleep so much?" he asked Karen.

It was only one of many questions Con asked that

morning. By the time the social worker left, Robbie had fallen in love with him all over again. He was so determined to learn everything he could to care for this child. A child he'd taken into a heart he didn't believe he had.

And Robbie had fallen in love with Joey all over again, too. She'd held his tiny body against her breast and known she'd made the right decision. The only decision. Unrequited love for Con was a small price to pay for the right to call this baby her son.

THE DNA RESULTS still weren't in by his wedding day. Con was glad he hadn't told Robbie about the possibility of having the boy for the weekend. She'd have been hugely disappointed. And one of them with dashed hopes was enough.

Con thought about canceling the wedding. There was no reason to put Robbie through this mess until he knew for sure Joey was his. Except that he *did* know. The boy had his chin.

And Robbie knew, too. Aside from the other reasons she'd listed for wanting to get married, she had her heart set on being Joey's mother. And he couldn't think of anyone he'd rather have help raise his son.

She was already at the church when he arrived. He knew she was there because he heard her swearing when he walked by the room she was using to change. Her colorful tirade was followed by a soft admonition from Susan. A half grin cracked Con's usually austere features as he continued on his way to the vestibule.

Robbie was still Robbie. Even on her wedding day.
He found something very reassuring about that.

He made it through the half hour before the wedding with relative ease. When he'd donned his rented tux that afternoon, he'd cloaked himself with the same numbing control he wore to work every day, and it stood him in good stead. This whole affair was merely a formality. Another undercover operation. He was confident he'd get through the day just like he did any other.

Until he was standing alone with the minister at the front of the church, that is, and saw Robbie and Stan coming up the aisle toward him. He didn't know which threw him more—Robbie looking radiant in her stunning white suit, or Stan, dressed in a black tux similar to Con's, smiling at him encouragingly. Robbie was going undercover with him—he could almost overlook her disguise—but Stan didn't know they were only playing a game. The older man's consummate acting could only be attributed to the great wealth of love he had for his daughter.

"Ladies and gentlemen, we are gathered here today..." The ceremony began.

Con answered the right questions in all the appropriate places, holding himself apart, an outside observer. Other than one glance at Susan, he didn't look at the audience—comprising, he knew, a few colleagues and friends—and he didn't look at Robbie again. He couldn't stand the pretense between them.

But he did make a vow during those moments that

he intended to keep till death did they part. He was going to protect his friend; he was going to make damn sure that this marriage didn't hurt her, that she'd have whatever freedoms her heart desired. And he was going to ensure that the marriage ceremony his drunken one-night stand had forced on them was not going to ruin the only good relationship he'd ever had.

"You may kiss the bride."

Con froze. He couldn't kiss Robbie. He couldn't even look at her.

Why hadn't they thought of this, prepared for it? Scratched it from the ceremony?

"Go ahead, Mr. Randolph," the minister whispered, accompanied by a few snickers from behind them.

He turned his gaze to Robbie and was thrown by the vulnerable look in her eyes. For some reason this mattered to her. And then it hit him. Her friends and loved ones were all watching. They thought this marriage was for real. And he *needed* everyone to believe it was for real.

Keeping his mental distance, his professional impartiality, Con lowered his head to hers.

And for a split second forgot they were Robbie's lips beneath his. Surprised at how soft, how womanly she felt. He moved his mouth against hers automatically, deepening what he'd intended as an impersonal gesture into something far more intimate. Her lips parted and he took her invitation instinctively, until he heard the minister's discreet cough.

This is Robbie! What in the name of God am I doing?

He jerked his mouth from hers. "I'm sorry," he whispered, unable to meet the shocked look he knew he'd see in her eyes.

He couldn't believe he'd done that. Robbie was his friend.

He escorted her down the aisle, stood beside her in the small reception line, accepted the congratulations of his colleagues and hers as they filed by. He even managed to be cordial to Karen Smith, to put his arm around his new wife and pretend that he and Robbie had married for the usual reasons. But he never looked at Robbie.

Until he saw the couple at the end of the line, speaking with Susan and Stan. Then he leaned over to ensure that his words reached only her ears. "You invited Pete and Marie."

"You never actually said not to."

"I told you I didn't want them here." It was hard enough getting through this charade, putting Robbie through it, lying to her parents, allowing her to lie to them, without this. *Yeah, Pete, my man, you're absolutely right. I'll sacrifice anyone, including my only real friend, in order to get my man. Or in this case, my son.*

"But you never came right out and said don't invite them."

They were heading toward him, a striking couple with Pete towering over his petite dark-haired wife. Con held out his hand to his sometime partner, thankful to Robbie for one thing. She'd made him angry as hell, wiping out all traces of the bizarre moment in front of the altar.

"Con. It's good to see you, man," Pete said, his grasp firm. Pete was a professional arbitrator, and Con had to hand it to him. He did his job well. Con almost believed Pete meant the words.

"Congratulations, Con. I'd hoped the love bug would get you," Marie said, standing on tiptoe to kiss his cheek.

"You're looking good, Marie," Con said, focusing on her pretty features rather than her words. She looked nothing like the tense unhappy woman she'd been when he'd first met her.

"Yes, well—" she glanced shyly up at Pete "—we're expecting again."

"Congratulations!" Robbie said, hugging Marie. The two had met only once before. It was at Pete and Marie's wedding when Con had had to show up as part of a couple or be assigned to some bridesmaid, but they'd hit it off right from the start.

"Wait'll you hear Con's news—" Robbie began.

"Not now, *dear*," Con interrupted, jabbing Robbie in the side. He wasn't ready to hang out more of his dirty laundry. *Hey, Pete. You know the night I got that woman killed? I also impregnated a woman whose name I didn't know, a woman I don't even remember screwing.*

Robbie glared at him—he'd probably bruised her ribs on top of everything else—but she let the moment pass, smoothing things over for him as Pete and Marie promised to talk with them later.

Robbie saw them through the small reception following the ceremony, as well, showing everyone that theirs was a match made in heaven. She made jokes about his terser-than-normal attitude, convincing their guests he was simply a very impatient bridegroom. He played along as best he could—and was eternally grateful to her.

Not that he told her so. He didn't know how.

CHAPTER SIX

IT WAS OVER.

Back in shorts and a tank top, her wedding suit safely tucked away, Robbie looked around her empty apartment one last time. Her truck was loaded with everything she was keeping, and Con was waiting outside to drive her home.

Home.

Why was it that Con's place had always felt like home—until today? She searched the floors of her bedroom closets. Empty. She knew they were. Con had already double-checked everything for her— every cupboard, every shelf. She was stalling. There was nothing of hers left here.

It was just that she wasn't sure there was anything for her at Con's house, either. She felt awkward moving in there, having no place of her own to run to when she needed to regroup.

And all because of that kiss. The second Con's lips had touched hers, everything had changed. She knew that was what was bothering her. Knew, also, that she couldn't talk to Con about it.

She used to be able to talk to him about anything. But she couldn't talk to him about that kiss, couldn't bear for him to learn that it had mattered so much to her, couldn't bear to see his pity. The only way she was going to get through this was to pretend she hadn't responded to him with such embarrassingly obvious passion, to act as though the kiss had been as meaningless to her as it had been to him.

If things were normal between them, she could have made him laugh about it, treated the whole thing like the joke it should have been. But she had a scary feeling that things weren't ever going to be normal between them again. They'd only been married a few hours and already there was a chasm between them, forcing them apart.

She needed a cigarette.

SHE WASN'T ALONE again until much later that night when she was in her room, furiously making her bed. Con had helped her carry in all her things. He'd set up her water bed without complaining once. Moving and filling that bed was something he'd done for her many times before, though not usually without cursing her and her taste in mattresses a time or two. Even something so mundane was no longer normal. But she was moved in; she had her stuff in her own bathroom—and they'd accomplished everything without once mentioning that kiss.

Their wedding supper was nothing to write home about, but by the time they'd made it to the kitchen for some sustenance, she'd been ready to eat. They'd had tuna-melt sandwiches followed by a companionable after-dinner cigarette. They were both still wearing the shorts and shirts they'd put on for moving.

"I found a way to Cameron Blackwell," Robbie had told him. She'd been so caught up in wedding plans she'd forgotten to tell Con about her coup.

"Yeah?" He didn't sound like he believed her.

"I made friends with his dog."

"You what?"

"I spent part of the weekend hanging out in front of his place, you know, just thinking, getting the lay of the land, trying to figure out the best way to approach him—"

"You were trespassing, just waiting for him to show so you could pounce on him," Con interrupted.

"Yes, well, his dog showed," Robbie continued, "and we got to know each other."

The look Con sent her was piercing. "Where'd he bite you?"

She was enjoying the cigarette much more than she should be. But at least it had come from Con's pack.

"That part's not important, Con. It wasn't deep. It just bled a lot. And while I was waiting for the bleeding to stop, we got to talking. Cameron's really a funny guy, Con. I liked him."

"Of course he's a funny guy. He writes comics."

"Just because he knows what's funny doesn't mean he's funny himself. Anyway, the main thing is, I'll get my story."

"He agreed to an interview? Because you got caught trespassing?"

Robbie fiddled with her cigarette on the edge of the ashtray. "Not quite," she admitted. "He wasn't too happy about that. And I had to promise him the interview would be strictly regulated by him, that I wouldn't exploit him, but rather just get to know him a little better. Oh, and I promised not to tell anyone that he reads romance novels by the dozen."

"He what?" Con's gaze shot to her, a hint of humor in his usually somber eyes.

"He came running out of the house so quickly when he heard me scream that he still had the book he'd been reading in his hand. There was a whole wall of them in his study, too."

Con studied her. "And you threatened to make something of it."

Robbie shrugged. She was a reporter. She had an obligation to the citizens of Phoenix. "I simply told him he had a choice. I'd tell my story, which was definitely going to give the wrong impression as I had so little to go on—or I'd tell his."

Con's mouth quirked into the half grin she loved so well but saw so infrequently. "You're something else, Rob. I almost feel sorry for Blackwell."

Warmth spread through her at his approving tone. And she blasted herself for the response. How would she get through years living with this man if she was going to go around reacting like a besotted idiot to every little thing he said?

"Where'd the dog bite you, Rob?" he asked, suddenly serious.

Damn. She'd hoped he'd forgotten about that.

"It doesn't matter, Con. Really. It's fine."

"Then why avoid the question?"

"Look. I told you it doesn't matter. Now drop it."

"You don't play around with dog bites. Did you have your doctor take a look at it?"

Damn his persistence. She wasn't one of his suspects. "He had to look when he stitched it up, now, didn't he?" she snipped.

Con ground out his cigarette. "God, Rob. It needed stitches? Show me where he bit you."

She put out her cigarette, too. "No."

He stood up, towering over her. "I assume the dog had all his shots?"

"Yes."

"The wound could still get infected. Show me where he bit you." He'd come closer.

He wasn't going to give up. She knew that.

"Show me." He was standing right over her.

"Here. It's right here," she said, touching the underside of her right breast.

If she'd thought the location would shock him, embarrass him, get any reaction out of him at all, she was wrong. He didn't miss a beat. "Show it to me," he said, his eyes filled with nothing but concern. They could have been talking about her big toe.

Except they weren't. And she was too aware of it— even if seeing an intimate part of her body apparently moved him not at all.

"Come on, Rob. Let me look."

"Forget it, Randolph. My tits are my own." She got to her feet, pushed past him and ran to her room, closing the door behind her.

She needn't have bothered. He hadn't followed.

Angrily Robbie forced the sheet corners around the bulky water-filled mattress.

How dare he think, even for a second, that he had any right to see her breast? For *any* reason.

How dare he think his first intimate sight of her was only going to be because of a repulsive little wound? How dare he not even realize it *would* have been his first sight of her?

How dare he not have passion in his eyes?

Robbie's hands went limp, the sheet slipping away as she sank slowly to the floor. That was the real problem. Had been all day. She'd seen the distaste in Con's eyes when the minister had asked him to kiss her that afternoon. And the memory was killing her.

It was one thing to assume she didn't turn him on. It was another altogether to have proof.

She was hurting like hell and she didn't have a clue how to deal with it. Con had never hurt her before. Because she'd never before allowed herself to want something from him he couldn't give, never before allowed herself to hope he might someday want her.

She couldn't blame Con. He'd die for her if she needed him to.

She just didn't turn him on.

"Robbie?" His call was followed by a knock on her door.

Leaping up, she grabbed a sheet corner. "Come on in," she called. The best way to get through this was just to pretend nothing had changed between them. She had to go back to looking at Con without feeling the touch of his lips on hers, without thinking about his taste, without imagining his passion.

She just hoped it wasn't too late.

"I think we need to talk," he said, leaning against the doorjamb.

Not yet. She wasn't done forgetting yet. "Go away, Randolph."

"You just told me to come in." His head almost touched the top of the doorway.

She yanked her bright yellow comforter out of a box. "Now I'm telling you to go."

"I'm sorry, Rob. I screwed up. Big time. I just want you to know it won't happen again."

She couldn't look at him, couldn't let him see how much his words were hurting her. It wasn't his fault she hadn't been honest with him about the way she felt. It wasn't his fault she was in love with him. And it certainly wasn't his fault she was such a turnoff to men. "Forget it, Con. I have."

"Thanks," he said. "And, Rob? Keep a close eye on that bite," he added, and was gone.

To spend his wedding night alone. Robbie spent the night trying to pretend that it was sweat and not tears soaking her pillow.

CON WAS UP EARLY the next morning. By the time he heard Robbie's bathroom door open, the homemade biscuits were just coming out of the oven, and the bacon and potatoes were done. It was time to put on the eggs, stay busy, not think about her somewhere in his house getting ready for the day. She'd spent the night here before—such as that time he didn't want her driving home in a monsoon and one night when she'd had too much to drink. And each time, she'd gotten up the next morning, too. There was nothing to it.

Except that she had stitches on the underside of her right breast. She'd have to be careful not to get them wet when she bathed. He spent the next several seconds thinking up different ways to keep them dry. Because he was worried about infection. That was all.

Breaking a yoke, he swore, then lit a cigarette, reminding himself of his game plan once more. He wasn't sure what he and Robbie were going to do with the day, but whatever it was, he would make up for the ass he'd been the day before. Starting with breakfast.

Susan had invited them to drive up to Sedona for a cookout later in the day, and Con wasn't averse to that. He'd be just as happy at home, working in the yard, but he'd made up his mind to do whatever Robbie wanted to do—and to be a good sport about it. Anything to get that hurt look out of her eyes. To get things back to normal. He should never have kissed her the way he had at the wedding. It was unforgivable.

And he could hardly stand to think about his moronic insistence she strip in front of him. When he'd heard that the dog had bitten deep enough to require stitches, he'd gone a little nuts. Dog bites were serious. He'd seen a guy with rabies once. He sure didn't want to lose Robbie that way. Or any other way.

"Mmm, smells good," she said, coming into the kitchen, her hair still wet from the shower. She picked up Con's cigarette, helped herself to a puff, then put it out. "If I had time, I'd make you give me some of that." She was watching him flip the eggs he was making for her.

"You going somewhere?" he asked.

She snatched a piece of bacon. "I'm covering the Fourth of July celebration at Patriots Square."

"I thought you had the rest of the week off."

"I called Rick this morning. Told him I could work." She chewed on the bacon as if she hadn't a care in the world.

Con's eyes narrowed. "Didn't he find it odd that you'd want to work the day after your wedding?"

"He assumed you had to go in."

Con lit another cigarette. "What about your parents' cookout?"

"I called them, too, told them we'd try to make it up there over the weekend."

She didn't want to spend the day with him. Maybe that was best.

"When do you expect to be back?"

She shrugged. "I don't know. Later."

Con ate their breakfast alone.

HE WAS THE ONLY ONE in the neighborhood doing yard work. Not many people celebrated the holiday that way. Which was fine with him. He had the world to himself as he clipped and trimmed, no friendly neighbors coming over to chat. Con hated it when they did that. He never had anything to chat about.

He finished trimming the bougainvillea bushes lining his wall, checked the irrigation on the fruit trees and wondered if Robbie would be home in time for dinner. Then berated himself for caring. He'd been eating dinner alone most of his life. If Robbie happened to stop over, it was no big deal. He'd never counted on it. Never needed it. He wasn't about to start now.

"I figured I'd find you back here."

Con swung around to find Stan Blair standing there. A good four inches shorter than Con, Robbie's father was still a big man, an intimidating man. Especially if you happened to have just married his daughter.

"Stan! Something wrong?" Con asked, his sheers hanging from his fingers.

"Not that I know of. I just wanted to talk. You got a few minutes?"

Con dropped his sheers on the growing pile of brush and headed toward his back door, grabbing the towel he'd left on a lounge by the pool on his way.

"Come inside," he said, wiping the sweat off his face and neck. "Where's Susan?"

"I left her at the mall. Dilliard's is having a sale."

He'd gotten rid of Susan. This talk was going to be serious. Con pulled a couple of bottles of beer out of the refrigerator and handed one to Stan.

"Thanks." The older man took the beer, but didn't open it right away. Setting it down on the breakfast bar, he excused himself to go to the bathroom.

Con watched as Stan left the room, a hard knot of regret in his gut. If this were a perfect world, if a kid had the right to choose his father, Stan would have been a good choice for him. Not that Stan would have seen it that way. Con had always been a pain in Stan Blair's ass.

He'd known that Robbie's father wouldn't have been happy about the wedding. But what could he possibly have to say about it now, after the fact?

Taking his beer with him, Con headed to the back of the house, as well, thinking he'd use this chance to clean up a little, at least change his sweat-soaked T-shirt.

His heart sank when he rounded the corner. Stan was in the doorway of Robbie's room looking at his daughter's unmade bed. Con's door was open across the hall, leaving a clear view of his own unmade bed.

Though Con would have liked to turn around and head right back to the kitchen, it was too late. Stan had heard him. So he continued down the hall, beer in hand, and stopped beside his father-in-law, staring at the incriminating bed, the single head print on the feather pillow.

"I'd hoped that things had changed," Stan said sadly, his gaze not leaving the bed.

Con wasn't sure what Stan meant. But he was pretty damn sure he didn't want to know. He stood silently, waiting.

"The wedding was for the boy, wasn't it?"

"Yes."

"You don't love her."

"I care for her."

"You've always cared for her, son. But she needs to be loved."

Con stood there looking at that lonely bed and nodded. He couldn't argue with Stan. The man was right.

"I'd hoped you'd learned to love her."

"Don't." Con took a swallow of his beer. There was no point in any of them setting themselves up for disappointment.

Stan shook his head. "She's special, my Robbie. Strong as they come, but soft and warm underneath. She'll make a good wife."

"I know."

They continued to stare at the bed. Con figured it was better than looking at each other. Stan had more to say.

"She deserves better than this."

Con nodded. So far, Stan wasn't telling him anything he hadn't already told himself.

"Did you ask her to marry you?"

"What do you think?"

Now it was Stan's turn to nod. "How long's it for?"

"As long as it takes. Maybe sooner."

"How long does *she* think it's for?"

Con didn't want to answer that. He didn't like the answer. "Forever, maybe."

Stan gave Con a sharp look. "I thought you were a better man than to use her like this."

Con doubted that, but the accusation still stung. "They're giving her a hard time down at the station, not including her in things. The guys are all married now. Their wives don't like them hanging out with a single woman."

Stan only grunted.

"She says she's lonely."

"So how's she going to find a husband to take care of that when she's married to you?"

Con didn't have an answer.

"The minute she called today, I knew there was trouble," Stan said, shaking his head. "I thought maybe you two had had a spat, figured it might take her a little while to adjust to having a man around telling her what to do. I had no idea it was this bad."

"I don't tell Robbie what to do." Con wanted that clear.

"Yes, well, maybe you should. Maybe if you had to make decisions for her, you'd love her."

Con could have told Stan that he liked Robbie just the way she was, that any man who tried to change

her didn't really love her, that pushing Robbie around
would not only be futile, but wrong. Except that the
information was irrelevant. All Stan really cared
about was whether or not Con loved Robbie.

But Con didn't love anybody. Stan knew that. God
knows he'd tried. His birth parents had never even
given him a chance. When he'd been young and na-
ive, he'd done everything he could to please his foster
parents, to love them as they'd expected him to. It
had never been enough, though. They hadn't been
able to love him, not after the years of trouble he'd
given them.

"I want a promise from you, son," Stan said, as if
reaching some conclusion.

Con stood silently, bracing himself to disappoint
Robbie's father again.

"I want you to stay away from her."

What kind of request was that? "We live in the
same house," Con said, tamping down his anger.

"You seem to have managed it last night." Stan's
tone was testy as he motioned toward his daughter's
bed and then to Con's own unmade bed across the
hall.

Con's jaw tightened as understanding dawned.
Robbie was thirty-three years old, and Stan was still
worried about Con getting into her pants. Because of
Stan as much as Robbie herself, Con had never ever
thought of Robbie in those terms. She was too special
to him. But Stan had never understood that. Con was
done hoping he ever would. And it was no longer any

of Stan's damn business whether or not Con had sex with his daughter.

"We're married," he said at last.

Stan turned, pinning Con with a glare that had been intimidating criminals for decades. "You touch her, you'll hurt her. I want your word, boy."

It was when he saw the despair in the older man's eyes that Con capitulated. Stan Blair adored his only child. He was trying to protect her from the pain of a loveless marriage; sex added to the equation would only intensify the pain.

The words stuck in his throat, but he finally said, "You have it."

Stan continued to study him doubtfully. Con thought he knew why.

During Con's junior year in high school the football coach's daughter had accused Con of forcing her to kiss him. The truth was Mitzy had gotten drunk at a party, thrown herself at him and been furious when he'd refused her. But the coach, a man Con had admired almost as much as he'd admired Stan, had believed otherwise. Con had been cut from the football team. And warned about the penalties for sexual assault.

"I never touched Mitzy Larson," he said through gritted teeth.

"I know that, son." Stan's leathery brow was still creased. "I was just thinking about Susan. I don't want her to know about this." Stan motioned to Robbie's room once more. "I don't want her worrying."

"Fine," Con said, wondering if Stan was telling the truth.

Stan's gaze fell and he seemed to study the toes of his tennis shoes. "I, uh, would rather Robbie not know I know, either. I'd like at least to salvage her pride."

"Fine," Con agreed again. He had no intention of talking to Robbie about sex again. Ever.

Without another word, Con turned and headed into his room. He was going to shower. Stan could wait or let himself out. It was no concern of his. All he knew was that he couldn't shake the image of that single imprint on Robbie's pillow.

CON WAS JUST SITTING DOWN to watch the ten o'clock news that evening when Robbie got home.

"Oh, good, just in time," she said, kicking off her sandals before she curled up on the opposite end of the couch.

He bit back a sarcastic remark. It wasn't her fault he'd been worried about her, or that he'd rather have had her company for dinner than eat alone. It wasn't her fault he was strangely aware of her bare feet on the couch between them. "Tough day?" he asked.

"Not too bad." She sounded too damn cheerful. And was that all she was going to tell him about what she'd been doing for the past twelve hours, after he'd spent the entire day thinking about her?

She reached for his cigarette, but he pushed her hand away, taking a drag himself.

"My, my, aren't we testy?" she drawled.

The news was just coming on and Con turned up the volume. He lit a second cigarette and handed it to her before he settled back to watch. It felt good having her home.

ROBBIE WATCHED the news as intently as she always did, but instead of listening to the stories being reported, which she already knew, anyway, she concentrated on the female announcer, Megan Brandt, noting her every expression, every nuance in her voice, every tilt of her head. Now there was a woman.

"I could do that," she finally said, leaning forward to flick the ashes off the end of her cigarette.

"I never knew you wanted to." Con was staring at her, his gray eyes curious.

Robbie shrugged. "Sure I want to. I hadn't planned on doing the grunt work all my life."

"You don't do grunt work." He turned back to the television and Robbie breathed a sigh of relief. Another few seconds under his penetrating gaze and she was going to forget that he wasn't supposed to have the ability to fire her blood.

"How're the stitches feeling?" he asked in the middle of a story about a car chase that had resulted in the arrest of two teenagers.

"Fine." Oh, Lord, they weren't going to start that again, were they? "I get them out Saturday." There, that should take the concerned look off his face. She could have told him they itched like hell, too, but she was damned if she'd discuss the condition of her breast with Con!

He nodded, his gaze on the TV again.

She turned her attention back to Megan Brandt, as well. She was going to concentrate on a dream that was feasible—to someday be the one reporting the news, not the drone collecting it. She couldn't make it through too many more days like the one that had just passed, picturing Con's face every time she closed her eyes, feeling his lips against hers every time she took a drink, driving herself crazy wanting to hurry home to him.

Only fools wasted their lives hoping for something they'd never have. And Robbie Blair Randolph was no fool.

CHAPTER SEVEN

HE EMPTIED his carton of milk in two swallows, never taking his eyes off Randolph's house as the woman came outside just after dawn Friday morning. She was wearing an old pair of cutoff sweatpants and a Phoenix Suns jersey. And she had legs that reminded him of the women he drooled over in magazines. Things were looking up.

He hadn't thought Randolph was screwing the woman all these months, although truth be told he didn't know a lot about screwing. Not nearly as much as he'd like to. But he'd seen them move a bunch of stuff in Wednesday night. And he'd been watching the house ever since, even slept in his car just around the corner the past two nights so he could stay close. He wanted to make sure he wasn't jumping to conclusions. And his vigilance had paid off. He'd been right. She'd moved in. They must be screwing.

This changed things of course. It would be longer than he'd originally figured before he could make his move. He'd have to work out another plan, take things real slow. Getting her out of Randolph's house was going to be tough. He couldn't afford any mistakes.

But he could wait. Now that he'd found a way to nail it to Randolph, to make him bleed, to hurt him so badly death would seem like a blessing, he could wait.

The woman bent down to get the newspaper on Randolph's driveway, and for a moment all he could see was her ass, pointing right at him. Now there was an ass Randolph would miss. A lot.

He could already taste victory. And it was sweeter than he'd imagined.

THE CALL CAME at seven o'clock Friday morning. Con and Robbie were in the kitchen, sharing the newspaper, a cigarette and a pot of freshly brewed coffee. He was already dressed for the yard work he'd left undone the day before, in cutoff jeans and a T-shirt. She hadn't yet changed out of the cutoffs and jersey she'd slept in.

Robbie was in the process of reminding herself that Con was her husband in name only, that the way his chest filled that T-shirt was no business of hers, when the phone rang.

"I'll get it," she said, dashing into the living room. It was probably Rick. After the way she'd been ogling Con for the past half hour she *hoped* it was Rick. She'd told her boss to call her if he came up with anything else she could cover during the remainder of her days off.

"Mrs. Randolph?" Robbie's stomach fluttered

when she realized the person on the other end of the line was addressing her. That she *was* Mrs. Randolph.

"Yes?"

"This is Sandra Muldoon, from social services."

"Yes?" she said again. Oh, God, it sounded as if Mrs. Muldoon had bad news. Had something happened to Joey? Please, let their baby be all right!

"We just received the results of the DNA testing, Mrs. Randolph." The woman paused. Robbie's skin went cold.

"And?" she asked, forcing her voice to remain calm. What if, after all they'd been through, they told Con that Joey wasn't his? Whether he acknowledged it or not, Con already loved that boy. And, Robbie suspected, loved having a son. A family he could call his own.

"Mr. Randolph is the boy's father."

Tears stung Robbie's eyes and her body went limp. It took everything she had to remain standing, to remember that Sandra Muldoon was still on the line, to keep from running back in to Con, throwing herself in his arms and bursting into sobs of joy. They had their proof. Nothing had gone wrong with the test. The court could not contest Con's fatherhood.

"Are you there, Mrs. Randolph?"

"Yes, ma'am. Thank you so much for calling. How soon can we see him?"

"Today," the woman said crisply. "The court approved an unsupervised visit for the weekend dependent on conclusive DNA results. I'd like to bring him by within the next hour. I trust you can arrange your schedule accordingly?''

"Great!" she cried. *Today! Our baby's coming today!* "I mean, yes, our schedule is fine!" And then more calmly, "We'll be ready."

SHE DROPPED the phone back in its cradle just as Con came into the room. He'd heard her holler.

"What's up?"

Robbie hurled herself at him, her arms encircling his neck. "We get him for the whole weekend, Con!" Her eyes shone. "The tests are back. Joey's your son!"

Con felt the shock of her words clear to the bone. And then was hit by a joy unlike he'd ever known before. The boy was his.

"He's mine." He needed to say it aloud.

Robbie was still hanging on to him. "Congratulations, Daddy!" she said.

He froze. *Daddy*. He had a son. A family. For the first time in his life he really belonged to someone.

Unfamiliar with the feelings drowning him, unsure what to do with them, Con pulled Robbie close, gazing down into her smiling face, her smiling eyes. And filled with self-hatred and despair, with selfish pride and joy, he lowered his mouth to hers.

WAVES OF PLEASURE coursed through Robbie as Con's lips touched hers.

Yes! her heart cried. Pent-up desire flooded her, almost frightening in its intensity.

Her mouth opened to him automatically, inviting him to deepen the kiss, allowing their tongues to mate. And then, in a flash, her befuddled brain remembered what had happened that last time he'd kissed her—the distaste she'd seen in his eyes.

For a split second, wanting him so badly she hurt, she considered ignoring the memory. But not at the risk of having him reject her again. She pulled out of his arms before he came to his senses. Because come to his senses he would, and she couldn't stand a repeat of their wedding day. Not today. Today was too perfect, too precious. Today they'd have Joey all to themselves.

"He's going to be here in an hour," she said, rushing over to pick up the FBI newsletter he'd left on the coffee table. She carried it to the desk he used to pay bills.

Con remained where he was, a dazed look in his eyes, and if Robbie hadn't been having such a hard time keeping her own emotions under control, she would have run right back to him.

"Robbie, about just now, I'm—"

"Forget it, Randolph. I'm happy, too," she interrupted him before he could say he was sorry a second time for kissing her. She straightened the cushions on the couch.

"He'll be here in an hour?" Con asked. She could feel him watching her, but he'd covered himself with his cloak of control again. It was in his voice, in the stillness of his body, as he stood in the doorway.

Robbie nodded. "There's nothing out in the kitchen he can hurt himself on, is there?" she asked. This would be a whole lot easier if Con would get busy, get away from her, give her a few minutes to recover.

She didn't know which was worse—only imagining his kisses, or these brief incomplete tastes of them. She just knew she needed his big sexy body out of her sight.

It wasn't to be. "Look at me," he said.

Robbie did as he asked, praying that she appeared convincingly unaffected.

"I didn't pull your stitches, did I?"

"No." She forced herself to meet his gaze. If discussing her breast didn't affect him, it certainly shouldn't affect her. Except that it did.

He studied her, frowning. "You sure you're okay?"

"Positive. Just a little nervous," Robbie admitted, surprised to realize that last part was true. She might not be much in the wife department, but she was going to be a mother in a little less than an hour. And that she was going to get right.

Con nodded, apparently satisfied. She wasn't sure if that was because she'd done a good job of hiding her feelings, or because he was distracted by Joey's impending visit. Either way, she was thankful.

He went around the room picking up ashtrays—

from his desk, the coffee table, an end table beside his recliner.

"Does this mean you won't be smoking this weekend?" she asked, wishing he'd have one last cigarette before Joey arrived. She could use a puff.

"*We* won't be," he said on his way out the door.

"What do you mean *we?*" Robbie called after him. "I quit."

CON FELT LIKE he was setting off for the Academy all over again. He figured they were going to find him wanting, knew they'd be right in their assessment and was determined to make it, anyway. He'd conquered the Academy. But somehow he knew that fatherhood was going to be a much bigger challenge.

"That's everything, then," Mrs. Muldoon said, clearly not very happy about leaving Joey in their care. "His schedule's written out there for you—" she gestured at the papers she'd handed Robbie "—along with the name of his doctor. And his foster mother packed a couple of jars of food along with a list of things he likes and doesn't like."

"Thank you," Con and Robbie said at the same time. Robbie began reading the schedule.

The social worker glanced again at the baby carrier Con held, her eyes wary as she watched the child sleeping inside. "Make certain you keep his blanket with him at all times," she said, turning toward the door.

"This dirty rag?" Con asked, indicating the dingy

scrap of white material clutched in the baby's fist. He planned to throw the damn thing out the first chance he got. And then go out to buy his kid a real baby blanket—something blue.

"It's clean, Mr. Randolph," Mrs. Muldoon said defensively. "Just well washed. It's been with Joey since he was born."

Which is far more than you've been. Con heard what the woman wasn't saying.

"No matter what changes life brings him, the blanket is one thing that doesn't change," the social worker explained, her face tight.

"It's his security blanket," Robbie said, looking up. "No problem. We'll take it with us everywhere we go."

Sandra Muldoon's back stiffened. "I hope you aren't planning to do much running around, Mrs. Randolph. Babies tend to be fussy when their schedules are disrupted."

"We'll take proper care of him, ma'am," Con said, moving toward the front door. He wanted the woman out of his house. Still holding the carrier with one hand, he opened the door with the other and wished Mrs. Muldoon a good weekend.

"You'll need to launder that outfit and send it back with him on Sunday. It's not his," she said as she stepped off the front step.

Looking at the one-piece green terry thing the boy had on, Con didn't see where it would be any real loss either way. But he'd send it back where it came from—along with an entire collection of outfits his son could call his own. It sickened him to think of the boy dressed in state hand-me-downs. Con had worn enough of the poor-fitting donated castoffs for both of them.

"We'll make sure you get it back," Robbie said politely just as Con was ready to tell Sandra Muldoon what she could do with her damn clothes.

"Be sure you drop him off at his foster parents' by six o'clock on Sunday." The social worker's parting words were clearly a warning. Almost as if Con was on probation. And in a way he supposed he was.

He'd just have to show Muldoon and her crew the stuff he was made of. And hope to hell the judge found something there that pleased him.

"What should we do with him?" he asked Robbie as soon as they were alone. "Just let him sleep?"

She glanced from the baby to Con and then back to the baby. "Yeah, but let's try and lay him in his crib," she said, leading the way.

For once, Con was satisfied to follow her, careful not to jostle the carrier against his leg as he walked.

Robbie kept glancing back at them, grinning. "You're really loving this, aren't you?" Con asked. It was hard to feel guilty about using her when she looked so damned happy.

"Yep. Now let's get our son to bed, Mr. Randolph."

He held the carrier over the crib mattress as Robbie slid her hands carefully beneath the baby's body and transferred him to the bed. His small chest shuddered, his chin puckering like he was going to cry, and Con held his breath. He didn't think it would be a good omen if the first thing they did was make Joey cry.

"Ssshhh," Robbie crooned, lightly rubbing the baby's back while she tucked his old scrap of blanket under his cheek.

With a huge sigh coming from one so small, the boy settled back to sleep. Con held his breath for another few seconds, waiting, watching. And feeling such a mixture of hope, pride and insecurity it was almost scary. He couldn't let his entire life depend on the boy, didn't dare count on making a home with his son no matter how much he wanted to. Because to count on it and lose would probably kill him.

"He's beautiful, isn't he?" Robbie whispered, resting her hand on Con's shoulder as she stood beside him looking down at the baby.

"Boys can't be beautiful, Rob," he said.

"He's too young to be handsome," she persisted.

"He isn't beautiful."

"How about gorgeous?" She was grinning down at the baby, her eyes glowing with love, and Con could have told her what gorgeous was. It was a woman with a heart so big she'd tied herself to a man who'd never love her, to a child she might never get to keep, and was happy, anyway.

"Or there's precious," she said. "A guy can be precious when he's still a baby, can't he?"

Con nodded, her nonsense working its magic. He

might not be a particularly nice man. He might not be a lovable man. But he was going to try his damnedest not to fail this new family of his.

"Having him here makes it all worth it, doesn't it, Con?"

He didn't answer. As much as he would have liked the cop-out, he didn't believe that having a son of his own was worth irresponsibly impregnating an emotionally unbalanced woman. It certainly wasn't worth the death that had started this whole chain of events. And he wondered if being sent a son was God's way of making sure he never forgot how badly he'd sinned.

The good Lord could have saved himself the effort. That woman's cries of fear, the blood soaking her blue dress and the role he'd played, were things that, with or without Joey, Con would remember every day of his life.

"He's family, Con. We're a family now," Robbie said. She was no longer looking at the baby. She was looking right at him, and Con didn't have to wonder what she was thinking. He could tell by the steely determination in her eyes.

"Don't count on it, Rob," he warned. What judge was going to give a child over to a guy who "got his man at any cost?" A guy so heartless he'd see an innocent woman die to close a case?

A guy who'd kissed his best friend not once, but twice? And the second time after promising her father, a man he greatly admired, that he wouldn't touch her.

"It's over Con. The past is over and done," Robbie said, her voice laced with the steel he'd seen in her eyes. "We've been given a chance for a new life here. All three of us. Let yourself take the chance, Con, please, or we'll all lose, you most of all."

If only it was that easy. To take a chance at happiness when he'd brought others so much pain. How could that possibly be right? He wished to hell he knew.

But he'd lost track of right and wrong a long time ago.

"Please let this work, Con. Let us be a family. For my sake and Joey's, if not for yourself," Robbie pleaded when he remained silent.

And suddenly Con felt the weight of his sins lifting a little bit. Robbie had done it again, had known just what to say to free him enough to reach for that elusive brass ring, after all. Not because he deserved it himself, but for Joey. And for Robbie. His son. And his wife.

AS HIS TRUCK ATE UP the miles from Sedona to Phoenix, Stan Blair chewed one of the antacids he'd given up when he'd retired from the Phoenix police force. Susan was humming and knitting beside him, transforming a ball of light blue yarn into a tiny sweater. She'd been humming ever since Robbie had called this morning, telling them they had the baby for the weekend. Susan couldn't have been happier. She was so eager to meet her grandson she asked Stan again and again how much longer it would be until they got there.

She'd made the trip countless times and certainly knew how long it took to get from Sedona to Phoenix. She was just urging him to drive a little faster. And had Robbie's marriage been normal—one based on mutual love, both physical and emotional—had he been on his way to meet the son of his daughter's loving husband, the son his daughter hoped to adopt, he'd have been pressing a little harder on the accelerator himself.

But he was filled with trepidation, instead. All he saw ahead was heartache. For everyone. Con and Robbie were crazy if they honestly thought they could make a celibate marriage work. And when it fell apart, they were all going to suffer. Susan, Robbie, himself. And Con and the boy, too. No one had a hope in hell of winning this one.

So why was he driving Susan straight into the biggest heartache she'd ever known? Why wasn't he turning their truck around, taking her back to Sedona and the emotional safety of their own home?

And telling her what? How could he explain any of this to her?

How could he tell Con Randolph he didn't believe in him? Because that was the message he'd be sending his reluctant son-in-law if he didn't show up on his doorstep as Robbie had asked.

It was a message he couldn't deliver. Because he did still believe—always had—that Con Randolph was a good man. He just didn't hold out much hope that Con would ever believe it.

"Come on, Stan, the speed limit's fifty here," Susan said when they turned north on Scottsdale Road from Bell. They were almost there. The antacid didn't seem to be working.

"I know what the speed limit is, dear," he said, reluctantly pushing the truck up to fifty.

A guy worked hard all his life, protected his family from harm, raised his kid to be a contributor to society. Was it too much to ask that he grow old with his family gathered around him happy and whole?

"Oh, Stan, she's outside waiting for us," Susan cried as he pulled onto Con's street. "And Con's with her. He's holding the baby. Oh, Stan, doesn't Con look happy?"

He didn't want to see. He didn't want to worry anymore. He didn't want to be there. Con didn't love Robbie. Their marriage wasn't made in heaven. And if something didn't change, they were all going to drown in a pool of tears before the year was out.

"Look, Stan!" Susan said again.

He pulled into Con's driveway, and Susan was out of the truck in a flash. This was it. He looked.

I'll be damned. His wife was right, or at least close to it. Con did seem happy as he held out his son to Susan's eager arms. At least as happy as Con ever seemed. His son-in-law wasn't smiling, but his eyes

were filled with a gentleness he'd never seen there
before.

Not as reluctant now, Stan got out of his truck.

CHAPTER EIGHT

CON WAS GLAD to have Stan and Susan around that first afternoon with Joey. With Susan oohing and aahing over the boy, it was a little easier for him to stand back, to distance himself enough to keep his bearings. It was a little easier to remember that Robbie wasn't a real wife. That they weren't the real family she was pretending they were. How could he forget with Stan there, watching with eagle eyes?

That was what Stan had always done. Con thought of the way he'd grabbed Robbie earlier that day, the way he'd kissed her to escape from himself. Just once he'd like to be worthy of Stan's trust.

Still, when the Blairs left shortly after dinner, he wasn't happy to see them go.

"You've got a boy to be proud of there, son," Stan said as they all walked out to Stan's truck. Robbie and her mother were trailing slowly behind, Susan holding Joey right up to the last minute. The boy had hardly cried all day. Which wasn't really surprising considering that he'd had two women hovering over him every minute, anticipating his every need, giving him more love in one afternoon than Con had probably had in his entire life.

"I can hardly take credit for him, Stan. I've just met him myself," Con finally said.

Stan stopped by the hood of his truck. "Part of you went in to making that boy, son. Nobody can take that away from you," he said before moving to the driver's-side door.

Con followed him, holding on to the door as the older man climbed inside. "I'm not going to let them take him," he said. He wanted Stan to rest assured that Robbie wasn't going to lose the baby she'd so clearly given her heart to.

"I know that, son," Stan said, putting his key in the ignition. "I'm not saying I condone any of this or that I take back what we discussed the other day, but you've made my daughter happy, and I thank you for that."

He pulled the door from Con's grasp and slammed it shut.

"Come on, Sus, I want to get off the highway before dark," he hollered, leaning over to open the passenger-side door.

Con stood beside Robbie as she waved her parents goodbye, Joey's arms and legs flailing against her.

"It's time for this little guy's bath," she said when her parents' truck was out of sight, forestalling any conversation Con might have had regarding their visit. Which was fine with him. There was no reason to tell her that her father had just thanked him for something for the first time in his life. Nor did she need to know how good that made him feel. He was sure it would pass.

ROBBIE AWOKE with a start and sat straight up in bed. She still wasn't used to sleeping at Con's house, and it took her a moment to get her bearings. Her gaze shot to the illuminated numbers on her digital clock. It was three in the morning.

The house was quiet. Maybe she'd only been dreaming. She was just lying back down, settling in to the soothing embrace of her water bed, when she heard it again. Con was talking to someone.

And that was when she remembered Joey. The baby was sleeping in his nursery across the hall from her. Or he was supposed to be. Was something wrong? Had Con had to call for help? Why hadn't he come for her?

Heart pounding, she was out of bed and across the hall in a flash. The baby's crib was empty.

She heard Con again, speaking softly, and followed the sound to the living room. She stopped at the doorway when she realized he wasn't talking on the phone after all. He was talking to Joey.

Robbie watched him with his son. The baby was in a corner of the couch propped up against a couple of pillows, probably from Con's bed, his blanket clutched in one tiny hand. And Con was standing behind the couch in the shirt and shorts he'd had on that day, holding a bottle to the baby's mouth. From where she was standing, Robbie could hear Joey's lusty sucking, could see, too, his wide-open eyes as he gazed up at his father.

Con's size didn't seem to intimidate Joey at all.

"You're a good boy, Joey," Con said, not in the tone an adult usually used with a baby, but as if he expected him to understand. "It's not your fault your life started off on the wrong foot. And don't you ever let anyone tell you any different. And don't you ever let anyone tell you I abandoned you, either. Because that's one thing I'll never do. You can count on it."

The baby continued to gaze up at him, his free hand resting alongside Con's on the side of the bottle. Robbie wasn't sure she'd ever heard Con string so many words together at once. He was anything but verbose.

He'd have been a lot more comfortable sitting on the couch with the baby in his arms, but she wasn't about to tell him so. He'd figure it out when he was ready. In the meantime she reveled in the pleasure of the moment. Seeing her husband bond with his son.

SATURDAY DAWNED an average Phoenix summer day, brilliant blue skies and temperatures expected to reach 120. Con and Robbie both awoke before the baby and were showered and waiting for him.

"I'll go check on him again," Robbie said when Con looked up from his newspaper for the third time in one article.

He nodded, having done the last check himself.

"He's still out," she said when she came back into

the kitchen. "But I checked his breathing and it's fine."

Con nodded again, taking a sip of his coffee. He'd rather have had a cigarette.

"Joey was up awhile in the night," he finally said. He wasn't sure why he'd admitted that, because he'd been thinking he'd keep their middle-of-the-night session between him and the boy.

"That explains the extra bottle in the dishwasher," Robbie said, surprisingly nonchalant.

Trust her to notice. "He was crying. I figured he might be hungry."

"He was probably wet. Did you change him?"

Did she honestly think he'd trust himself to do that on his own the first night? The boy was a hell of a lot different from the toy he'd practiced on. "No, but you put an overnight diaper on him."

Robbie picked up the baby's schedule Sandra Muldoon had left the day before. They were keeping it out on the breakfast bar where they could refer to it easily.

"It says here he's usually awake by seven. That's almost an hour ago," she said, reading on.

Con didn't like the sound of that. Was the kid coming down with something?

"But he doesn't normally eat in the night anymore. Maybe he's just sleeping late because his tummy's full."

Con sincerely hoped so. But he decided to go in

and feel the boy's skin, anyway, just to make sure he wasn't hot.

When he slipped quietly into the nursery, Joey was wide awake and gazing up at the mobile Robbie had hung over his crib, following the brightly colored race cars as the air-conditioning blew them gently in a circle.

The boy turned his head when Con approached, his fat cheeks dimpling as he grinned up at his father. Before he knew what was happening, Con felt himself grinning back.

"So you were playing possum with us, eh, boy?" he asked, lifting the baby out of the crib.

Joey kicked his feet against Con's stomach, gurgling at him.

And Con had thought *Robbie* was irritatingly cheerful in the morning. It seemed he was going to be surrounded with cheerfulness. In the years to come he'd probably have to get up at five in the morning just to have his few minutes of grouchiness in peace.

"Robbie!" he bellowed, carrying the baby to the changing table. Joey's sleeper was soaking wet. And now Con's shirt was, too.

Joey's chin puckered, his lips pursed, and his little face turned a mighty shade of red. And then he let loose with an ear-piercing wail.

"You scared him," Robbie said, running into the room.

"So it seems," Con snapped, picking the baby back up from the changing table.

"It's okay, guy, Daddy's just got a big voice." He held the boy to his chest and rubbed his back like he'd seen Robbie do yesterday.

And before he knew it, Joey was quiet, his hiccups the only evidence of the storm.

"He's soaked," Con told Robbie unnecessarily. She couldn't help but see that the entire back of the baby's sleeper was wet.

"Into the tub with you, young man," she said, taking him from Con.

Con followed her to the kitchen, where he set the plastic tub up in the sink and collected the tear-free soap and hooded towel. He had this down pat at least.

"He was wide awake when I went in," he told Robbie as he watched her bathe the baby. He didn't know how she managed to hold on to all those squirming slippery appendages.

"We need to get a monitor," she told Con over her shoulder. "Yes, that's a good boy," she cooed to the baby in the same breath. "You like that, don't you? Is Joey a happy baby? Say yes. Say yes. Come on..." Con wished the guys he worked with could see her now.

Except that he was kind of glad he was the only one seeing her this way. She was going to be a wonderful mother. To *his* son.

If they got custody.

Joey slapped his hand on the water, splashing Robbie, the counter and a brand new roll of paper towels.

Robbie laughed. "Oh! He's a strong boy, a very big boy to splash like that..."

Con found himself grinning again, whether at the baby or the woman he'd married, he wasn't sure. He fetched an extra towel and soaked up the puddles.

But he didn't feel at all like grinning a few minutes later when she lifted Joey from the bath. The baby's foot caught on the edge of her T-shirt, jerking it up above her breasts. The first thing he noticed was that she wasn't wearing a bra. And the second was that his best friend had incredible breasts. He suddenly couldn't breathe—and couldn't look away.

And then he saw the painful-looking gash on the underside of her right breast. It wasn't large, only an inch or so, but it angered him to see it there. He'd like to get his hands around the neck of the dog that did that to her.

"Let me take him," he said, lifting the baby from her arms. "Your stitches are getting wet." He didn't mean to sound so harsh, but dammit, she should be more careful.

And so should he about where he looked.

"It won't kill me," she snapped, turning her back on him as she yanked her shirt down.

Even as he held the squirming wet baby, Con couldn't get the sight of her out of his mind. He pictured himself touching her, tasting her. And castigated himself for his body's hot response. Robbie was his friend, and his son's mother.

He of all people had absolutely no business thinking of her as a woman.

Not only because he'd promised Stan he wouldn't or because he'd led Robbie to believe he wouldn't, but because he couldn't. When Con went to a woman for sex, sex was all it was. Period. To him, women were like a shot of bourbon. A quick fix, nothing more.

And he was damned if he'd reduce Robbie to that.

Joey's sudden wail brought his parents' attention back to him.

"He's cold," Robbie said, reaching over to wrap the towel more firmly around him. Her movements were jerky, awkward.

Holding the ends of the towel together, Con carried the baby into the nursery and placed him on the changing table.

"Let's see if I can get *this* right," he whispered to the boy, hoping Robbie was behind him to back him up.

She was. She was his coach, his judge and his part-time cheering section as he fumbled with flailing arms and legs, struggled with tape closures that insisted on sticking before he got both sides of the diaper around the baby's leg. But eventually he managed it. And eventually he dressed his son.

Almost as if sensing the importance of the occasion, Joey was a gracious participant, amusing himself with his toes throughout the entire event.

"What time's your doctor's appointment?" Con

asked Robbie an hour later as he rinsed Joey's cereal bowl. Robbie was wiping the baby's face and hands for what seemed the hundredth time.

"One o'clock." She felt the blood suffuse her face at the reference to those damn stitches. He'd seen the gash she'd been trying to keep from him, after all. And a whole lot more.

"We can pick up a monitor beforehand," Con said.

She pulled the baby from his carrier. "What do you mean, we?"

"I thought Joey and I would go along." His back was still to her. He seemed to be taking an awfully long time to rinse one little bowl and spoon. And suddenly Robbie understood.

"You're afraid to be here alone with him."

His back stiffened and his hands stilled. "I'm not afraid."

She held the baby up to her shoulder, rubbing his back. It wouldn't hurt to have them come along with her. "You'll have to keep him in the waiting room," she said. She wanted it clear that Con wasn't following her in while she had the stitches removed. He'd gotten the one good look at her breasts he was going to get in this lifetime.

"Fine." He turned around, suddenly done with his chore. "We should take your truck. It's bigger."

And that was when it hit Robbie that they had a problem, after all, in spite of their preparations. "We don't have a car seat."

Con stared at her silently for several seconds. "I'll

go get one.'' He grabbed his keys from the counter, checked to see that he had his wallet in the pocket of his shorts and started for the door.

Robbie waited.

He didn't even make it out of the room. ''What am I getting?'' he asked, turning back around.

''Just make sure it's a full-size infant seat, Randolph. Ask someone at the store to help you. And keep in mind that I'm going to be lifting the thing, too.'' She grinned at him.

Con nodded, then said, his jaw tense, ''I am not afraid to be alone with him.''

She turned the baby around, sitting him up on her lap. ''Sure you are, Randolph, but it's okay. Most dads are at first. It's perfectly normal.''

He left without another word.

''MRS. RANDOLPH?''

''Yes?''

Con's gaze flew to Robbie. *Mrs. Randolph?*

''The doctor will see you now.''

He didn't have time to fret about being left in sole charge of his son. He was too busy thinking about Robbie as Mrs. Randolph. Besides, with an office full of nurses and a waiting room full of women, he had plenty of backup.

Joey was sleeping in his new carrier-cum-car-seat, clutching his scrap of blanket. ''Just pick him up if he wakes,'' Robbie whispered to him as she stood to go.

Con nodded. He knew what to do. He was the one who'd heard the kid cry during the night. Well, Joey hadn't actually made it to the crying stage, but only because Con's senses were acute from years of training, and the whimper that would have become a cry had woken him from a sound sleep.

He'd been unsure what to do, unsure of his ability to give the boy what he needed. But considering the alternative—going into Robbie's room to wake her, being in the same room with her while she was in bed—he'd decided to deal with Joey himself.

At least Robbie was in the house, a sort of safety net. He could always go for her if he couldn't figure out what to do. But to his surprise, he'd done just fine.

Give him another couple of years and he might even be ready to tackle the kid without anyone else within yelling distance.

He glanced at Joey and then looked again. His son. His flesh and blood. He'd never met another soul in his life who had his bloodline, his genes. The boy was family.

Mrs. Randolph. He thought again of the nurse calling out the name. Of Robbie answering. He'd never given enough credence to the brief ceremony they'd enacted for their "undercover operation" to acknowledge that it had actually changed Robbie's name. Changed it to his. He supposed she was family now, too.

Joey was still sleeping when Robbie returned a few

minutes later. Con's brows raised in question, his gaze on her breast.

Robbie frowned at him, busying herself with the baby's things. "I'm fine. All healed. He doesn't even think there'll be a scar," she said, reaching for Joey's carrier.

"I'll get that," Con said, standing, as well. No scar. Maybe not, but he'd always know where one might have been.

Ten minutes later Con waited in the car with a still-sleeping Joey while Robbie ran into the store for the baby monitor. He turned the air conditioner up to maximum. It was 115 outside. He didn't want the boy sweating.

"It's freezing in here," Robbie said, shivering as she climbed back in the passenger side. They'd decided to take his car, after all. The car seat required a shoulder strap, which, in the truck, would have required Robbie to sit in the middle next to Con. They'd both reached the realization at the same time, and without either acknowledging why, they'd moved to the car, instead.

Con turned down the air, wondering if they'd ever regain the easy camaraderie they'd had before the wedding, before he'd blown things by kissing her. Before Stan had made such an issue of her big lonely bed.

Before someone had called her Mrs. Randolph. *Mrs. Randolph.* His wife.

He needed a cigarette. "You feel like a burger?" he asked.

"Sure." She fastened her seat belt, glancing in the back once more to check on Joey.

"You think he'll be okay if we eat it there?"

Robbie shrugged. "I don't know. Mrs. Muldoon said not to take him out too much. What do you think?"

They both looked at their sleeping charge. "I think we need to start as we mean to go on," Con said. He planned to take his son with him everywhere. At least, everywhere a kid could go.

"Then let's go get burgers. I'm starved."

ROBBIE FOUND CON leaning against a pillar outside by the pool that night after dinner. Smoking a cigarette.

"Damn," he said, putting the cigarette out when he saw Joey in her arms.

Robbie grinned. "Don't talk like that in front of the baby."

Con grimaced. "Sorry."

He looked grouchy. But he was trying so hard it broke Robbie's heart. She wished he trusted himself a little more.

"You want to go swimming?" Con asked suddenly.

A dip in the pool sounded like heaven. She'd been feeling too warm and clammy all day. "Yeah, I do," she said. "Here, take him while I change." She handed him his squirming son.

"We didn't get a suit for him," Con said, automatically settling the baby on one hip.

Robbie felt tears threaten as she watched him handle the baby. In just twenty-four hours he'd grown so much more comfortable with his son. "He can go in his diaper," she said.

Robbie ran inside and slipped into her sleek one-piece racing suit. She and Con hadn't swum together in ages.

Because the last time you did you drove yourself crazy lusting over his powerful chest, his hard-as-rock stomach, his long muscular legs, she reminded herself. But that wasn't going to happen tonight. She'd have Joey to concentrate on. She wouldn't even know his father was there.

And pigs fly.

CON AND JOEY had been in the water for quite a while when Robbie finally came out and dove into the pool behind him.

"How does he like it?" she asked, surfacing.

"He likes it just fine," Con said as she stood up in the shallow water. *And so does his father,* he thought. Why in God's name had he never noticed before what a great body Robbie had? And why was he noticing now? She, and her firm luscious breasts were off-limits. Period.

"Did he cry when you put him in?" she asked, watching as he bobbed the baby up and down.

"Nope."

She reached out to tickle the baby and Joey giggled.

"Omigosh! He laughed!" she cried, tickling the baby again.

And suddenly Con felt like laughing, too. Joey's delight in Robbie's attentions was contagious.

She grabbed the baby under his arms, swung him up in the air and brought him down to splash in the water. Joey shrieked with pleasure, and she did it again. And then again, both of them laughing.

Con had never found a woman so sexy.

He backed slowly away, into deeper water, hiding his erection. Robbie's breasts, straining against her suit as she lifted the baby, were a sinful temptation. He crossed to the other side of the pool and started to swim laps.

She was still playing with the baby when he'd exhausted his body to the point of numbness. But at least he'd be able to get out of the pool without embarrassing himself.

"I'm going in," he said, reaching the shallow end.

"Then take him, would you, so I can swim." She held the baby out to him.

He reached for the boy, unaware that Joey had a hold on the strap of Robbie's swimsuit. The baby's grip was strong, and when Con grasped him, together they pulled Robbie off balance. Her thigh brushed Con's, smooth as silk, firm, feminine.

And just like that he was on fire again.

She gasped and started to laugh again, grabbing Con's arm to steady herself, but Joey wouldn't let go of her. She fell against them, instead, her hips bumping Con's. He knew the very instant she felt his hardness.

The laughter died in her throat, her fingers dug into his arm, and her expression closed. She pried the baby's fingers off her suit.

Joey's little hand found a new target almost instantly—the mass of hair on Con's chest, which he clutched and pulled. Hard. Con had never been more thankful for pain in his life.

"No, no, Joey, you'll hurt Daddy," Robbie said softly, releasing the baby's fingers one by one.

Con's chest constricted beneath her tender touch, his nerve endings taunting him. Testing him. She knew what she was doing to him. And she was still doing it. She wasn't backing off.

But she had to. There was a very good reason she had to.

"You're a little rascal." She chuckled seductively as Joey, having discovered the fun to be had, tried for another handful of hair.

Her voice was husky, her fingers lingering against Con's skin suggestively as she once again loosened the baby's hand.

She was still the Robbie he'd always known. And

yet she wasn't. She was his wife. But not in the way that mattered. She couldn't be. He'd given his word.

He thought of the promise he'd made Stan. Of the reason he'd made that promise. He'd agreed to Stan's stipulation for one reason and one reason only. Because the old man was right. Robbie deserved much more than he could ever give her. She deserved love.

And all he had to offer her was sex.

"Enjoy your laps," he said abruptly, then twisted away from her, the baby in one arm, and climbed out of the pool. Joey's fingers found their mark again, yanking harder than he'd have thought a sixth-month-old baby could. Con didn't even flinch and continued on into the house.

He didn't place the baby in his crib, because he didn't trust himself not to head right back outside to his mother.

CHAPTER NINE

IT WAS QUARTER after five Sunday afternoon. The time Robbie had been dreading since she'd gotten up that morning. She looked at the big face of her men's digital sport watch again, hoping for a few extra minutes. But it was five-fifteen, not five-ten. They needed to leave by five-twenty at the latest if they were to have the baby back on time.

Con was asleep on the couch, Joey napping on his chest. Con's arm curved around the baby, his hand resting on the baby's back. They'd been that way for more than an hour, and the last thing Robbie wanted to do was disturb them.

But she was going to have to wake them, or wake Con, anyway. This was one instance when being late could mean life or death—at least for their dreams.

She arose from the chair she'd been sitting on for most of the past hour, tucking her T-shirt back into the blue-jean cutoffs she'd had on all day. She'd been strangely comforted by the steady rise and fall of Con's chest, the stern set of his chin, even in sleep.

As she approached the couch, her gaze traveled lower, to his long muscular thighs. She remembered the feel of those hair-roughened legs pressing against her in the pool yesterday, the rock-solid hardness of him as the water rippled sensuously around them.

He'd wanted her. For one brief moment he'd found her desirable. Until he'd looked at her. Until he'd realized whose body was pressing so intimately against his own. Then he couldn't have made it clearer that his response wasn't for her. But she already knew that. Had known it for years.

She'd swum forty laps before she'd followed him into the house, attempting to dispel the pain his rejection had left behind, to numb her buzzing nerve endings, to convince herself she wasn't as starved for the feel of a man's body as she thought she was. Con's body.

"Con?" she called softly.

He was instantly awake, his eyes alert, searching.

"It's time to go." She bent to take the baby, hoping to keep Joey asleep for a while longer. She didn't want him crabby when they returned him. She didn't want to give his foster mother any room for complaint.

Con stood up, his gaze averted from the baby. "I'll get his things," he said, leaving the room. Robbie watched him go, saw the stiffness return to his back, to his entire being.

This wasn't going to be easy. Not for any of them. She hugged the baby to her breast, breathing in his sweet scent. *We'll miss you so much, little Joey. If only there were some way for you to know how much we love you. And please, oh, please, don't forget us before we see you again.*

"Let's go." Con was back, his face a study in control.

They took his car again and the forty-minute drive to Gilbert was accomplished in total silence. Con was at his most unapproachable, his eyes flinty, his body more like a marble sculpture than flesh and blood. She wished there was some way she could reach him, ease the hurt and frustration that was causing him to retreat into the armored shell he presented to the world.

As each mile passed, the knot in her stomach grew, the pain in her chest making it harder and harder to breathe. After only two days she couldn't bear the thought of waking up without Joey, sitting down to eat without feeding him first, going to sleep at night without hearing his steady breathing on the monitor beside her bed.

She couldn't imagine having him in her arms one second and gone the next.

They passed the Gilbert city-limits sign, and Robbie closed her eyes. She didn't want to see the neighborhood, the peeling billboards and unmanicured lawns, to see pictures of the places Joey might already be familiar with, places he would recognize more easily than Con's home. Tears burned behind her eyelids and she willed them back. Tears weren't going to help.

Joey was still asleep when Robbie pulled him from

his car seat and carried him up to the door of the faded-wood house. Con followed silently with Joey's things, carrying an extra knapsack that contained a wardrobe of new outfits they'd picked up after their burgers on Saturday.

She'd wanted Joey to sleep, but now she hoped he'd wake up before they had to leave him so they'd at least be able to say goodbye to him. She hated the thought of his falling asleep with them and waking up with someone else. She didn't want him to think they'd abandoned him.

Betty Williams, Joey's foster mother, took the baby from Robbie's arms as soon as she opened the door.

"Good. You're right on time," she said, smiling as she looked down at Joey. "And he's sleeping, too. Hopefully it'll last another half hour. My family's right in the middle of dinner."

"Let's go," Con said to Robbie, setting Joey's things by the door before turning and heading back to the car.

Robbie couldn't just walk away and leave her little boy with this total stranger. "He's got some new clothes," she told the woman.

"Oh! Thank you." Mrs. Williams glanced over her shoulder, her hand on the front door. She obviously wanted to get back to her family.

"Well, if you have any questions about anything, call us. Our number's in there with his stuff."

"Fine," Mrs. Williams said.

"Mama!" A child's cry came from the interior of the house.

"Just a minute!" the woman called back.

Joey shifted, but he didn't wake up, as if sleeping through bouts of loud noise wasn't all that unusual.

"I'll let you get back to your dinner, then," Robbie said. She knew she had to go.

"Thanks for baby-sitting for us," Betty Williams called just before her door closed.

Robbie flinched as the words lashed her. *Baby-sitting?* Was that all she and Con were? Baby-sitters? People with no authority whatsoever in the decisions made in Joey's life? With no rights?

No! She refused to accept that. No matter what the state said, what the courts thought. They'd been a family this weekend, a real family. A mother, a father, a son.

The car was already running, with Con sitting impatiently behind the wheel. He threw it into reverse before Robbie even had her door closed. As much as she hated to cry, hated the weakness, the run-down neighborhood was blurred by her tears as they sped past. She'd just left a big piece of her heart behind.

Accelerating, Con pulled a pack of cigarettes out of the console, snapped open the ashtray and lit up, taking a long drag before offering the cigarette to her. Robbie accepted it gratefully and wiped away her tears with the fingers of her free hand. Con lit another cigarette for himself.

Angry control was in every movement he made.

He drove well, but not smoothly, accelerating more quickly than necessary, taking corners sharply, yielding to no one.

He said nothing about the child they'd just left behind.

A car with a bunch of teenage boys pulled out in front of them, forcing Con to brake or hit them. "Bastards," he said, slowing down.

Robbie held her tongue. She was sitting beside a stick of dynamite that was dangerously close to exploding.

"At least you can smoke again," she said lightly, worried about him. They had to get through this. They were probably going to have to get through a lot more before it was all over.

Con grunted.

Robbie fell silent again, watching the neighborhoods whiz past, the seemingly endless miles that were taking them farther and farther from Joey. In an emergency it would take them forever to get to him.

If he has an emergency, will we even be called?

The car jerked to a halt behind a woman in a blue minivan in the right-turn lane. The light was red, but there was no oncoming traffic. No reason the woman couldn't turn. Except that she was reaching behind her to an infant seat in the back. "Go," Con muttered, scowling.

Robbie fought a fresh welling of tears. "You had no choice, Con. You had to leave him there."

"Tell Joey that." He passed the blue minivan, accelerating from zero to the speed limit in seconds.

"I know it's hard, but we have to remember that the system is there to protect him," Robbie said. The system helped children every day, made their lives better, didn't it? Joey would be all right. He'd already survived six months without them.

"The system can go to hell."

In that moment Robbie had a hard time not agreeing with him. What kind of system would force a man to do something that went against every responsible bone in his body? Force him to turn his newfound infant son over to total strangers?

No matter how hard she tried to look for the positive, she just kept thinking about what Joey was going to think, how he was going to feel, when he woke up to find they'd gone. Would he be scared? Would he miss them? Cry for them? Or would he just shrug them off as another couple of the temporary adults who had passed through his young life?

Would he care that there'd be no race-car mobile for him to watch when he awoke in the morning?

JOEY'S THINGS mocked Con when he followed Robbie through the garage door into the kitchen half an hour later. Clean bottles stood upside down on a towel by the sink, a can of soy-milk powder beside them. A blue teddy-bear rattle had been abandoned by the refrigerator. And a soiled bib still lay on the breakfast bar.

"Why in hell didn't you put that in the laundry?" Con snapped, pointing at the offensive garment.

"I forgot. I'm sorry," Robbie said softly, picking up the bib, quietly sliding open the doors concealing the laundry closet and dropping the tiny garment into the washing machine.

"And what about the bottles?" he asked, glaring at them.

"I'll get them." She quickly removed the bottles and all other evidence of the baby from the kitchen.

What in hell was she doing? What in hell was *he* doing? *He'd* left those bottles there.

"No. I'm sorry, Rob." He ran his fingers through his hair, trying to make sense out of a world gone mad. "I just can't... It's not... I feel so..." He broke off, not knowing what he even wanted to say. He just knew that if he allowed himself to feel the waves of despair crashing around him, he'd drown. He had to keep fighting to keep them at bay.

"It's okay, friend," Robbie said, moving to him and squeezing his hand briefly. "I understand."

Which was more than he did.

"That still doesn't give me the right to take it out on you." She'd just changed her entire life for him, and he repaid her with a display of bad temper.

"That's what friends are for," she said, trying a grin that didn't quite work.

She was hurting, too. He could see the pain in her steady gaze, in the tremble in her chin. He put his arms around her and pulled her against him.

"Ah, Rob, what have we gotten ourselves into?" he asked.

"Just another one of life's little challenges, I guess." Her words were muffled against his chest.

Resting his chin on the top of her head, the short blond tendrils of her hair tickling his face, he told himself to set her away. But her warmth was too soothing. "We have to face the fact that the judge may not give him to me. To us."

She shuddered, pulling back to look up at him. "He has to, Con. And he will."

She must have seen Con's doubt. "Look at all we have to offer Joey," she added. "How could he not?"

Con grimaced. She'd never really seen him for what he was. "*You* have a lot to offer, maybe. *I* fathered a child with a woman I didn't know."

"You were drunk, Con."

"Oh, that makes it all right, then," he said sarcastically. He had to make her see the truth.

They might very well not get the boy. Con had a lot of strikes against him. Always had. And he couldn't have Robbie resting all her hopes and dreams on the chance that the judge was willing to overlook his mistakes, the flaws in his character.

"It makes you human, Con. Once you have a chance to explain the circumstances—"

He cut her off. "He'll certainly find it commendable that I was so bloodthirsty for Ramirez I allowed an innocent woman to die just to get him."

"You didn't know—"

"I knew *someone* was there," he said harshly.

She reached up and traced the lines on his forehead with gentle fingers. "But you thought it was an accomplice."

He needed to let her go. Out of his arms. Out of his life. He had nothing for her. Not even the baby she wanted so badly to mother.

"It doesn't matter what I thought," Con said. "I should have waited."

"And let Ramirez get away?"

"Why not ask the question of the family who loved that woman? Why not ask the teenage boy who had to make his mother's funeral arrangements, instead of attending his high-school prom?"

Robbie sighed and laid her head back on his chest. "You're a good man, Con Randolph. You have a good heart. Someday, somehow, I'm going to make you see that."

Con took Robbie's shoulders and held her away from him. Her belief in him was a burden he could no longer bear, not when it was leading her into pain and unhappiness. He couldn't let her stay another minute if she wasn't going to do it with her eyes open.

"I have no heart, Robbie. None."

Tears flooded her eyes as her lips formed a trembling smile. "Oh, yes, you do. You're just not listening to it yet."

Her refusal to see the truth was one frustration too many. "You're the one not listening, Robbie. It's time to give up the pretense." His grip on her shoul-

168 SHOTGUN BABY

ders tightened. "I'll never have these great qualities you think you see in me. And if you can't accept that, you need to get out."

Her eyes continued to shimmer with tears. "You have them, Con. I see them every time you risk your life to right an injustice. I feel them every time you look at me, every time I need a friend and you're there, every time you get mad at me for doing something a little dangerous."

God, the woman was obtuse. "I'm *using* you, Rob," he said brutally. He had to get her away from him, to protect her.

"You aren't using me. We're using each other. Otherwise known as caring. It's what being friends is all about."

Friends. Right. If he was any kind of friend, if he *cared*, his body wouldn't be on fire for her. Maybe, he thought next, that was the *only* way to get her see the truth. To *show* her how badly he could use her.

Even while his brain told him it was wrong, he gave in to the temptation that had been driving him mad for days. He hauled her to him and crushed her lips beneath his own. He didn't ask for a response, he took one, forcing her lips open. She wasn't his friend anymore. She was just a woman who had something his body wanted.

His tongue plundered her mouth, showing her none of the respect that had defined their relationship since they were kids. He let his desire lead him and didn't even attempt to soften its force. A part of him, some small speck left over from his boyhood, cried out, knowing he was destroying the one good thing he'd ever had in his life—Robbie's affection for him.

Her mouth was warm and soft, so deliciously soft. And her tongue was doing things to him that had never been done before.

He continued to ravage her mouth, trying to consume her. Except that she wasn't letting him consume anything. She was giving what he demanded and taking as much in return. Her tongue matched his thrust for thrust. She was a formidable opponent, better now than during the best of their verbal battles.

And suddenly Con couldn't do it. Couldn't take that final step that would make her hate him—and maybe herself, as well.

Confused, he pulled away. Something was happening. He just had no idea what. His body was still hard and throbbing, still wanting to drive into her, to seek satisfaction in the only way he knew. But his mind had suddenly taken a different route; he was thinking of the woman he held, not of the body he'd been about to plunder. He had no idea what was wrong with him, with her. He only knew he had to stop.

He moved back another step, steadying his breathing, willing his heart to resume its normal pace, until all that was left of the moment was the bitter aftertaste of shame.

"I've never forced a woman," he said. It was suddenly imperative she know that.

"I didn't think you had."

Her voice was husky. His body started to throb again. He had to put a stop to the insanity.

"What just happened," he said, "don't go thinking it meant something. It didn't."

She stood in front of him, her chest heaving with the effort it took to breathe. "It meant you want me."

Her boldness turned him on even more, making him desperate. "It meant I want sex. Who with isn't important. When it's time, I take what's offered."

He took no satisfaction when his barb hit home. She flinched and retreated a step. "I didn't offer."

"What do you call last night in the pool?"

She stared at him, stricken, speechless for the first time since he'd known her. For all her toughness she was as tender as they come, no match for him at all. He was winning hands down. So why did he feel so awful?

"Your nipples were hard as pebbles, babe, and you were playing with my chest like a woman in heat," he taunted, purposefully cruel—and hating himself for every word he said. But someday she'd thank him. Someday she'd be grateful he'd saved her from him.

"Why are you doing this?" she asked. Again her eyes shimmered with unwashed tears.

They were almost his undoing. Except that too much was at stake. Her own father knew she needed saving. "Why shouldn't I take what's offered if I feel like it? As I recall, you're my wife."

"Because this isn't how you do things, Con Randolph," she said, her chin trembling. "You may really be a cold, hard man, but you've never been cruel.''

She was supposed to be running from him in tears, not sounding like some damn righteous know-it-all. And his shorts weren't still supposed to be so painfully tight.

She stepped close to him again, her gaze steady as she looked into his eyes. ''You're trying to save me from myself, aren't you. It'd be just like you to do something so ridiculously outrageously noble—and stupid.''

Con issued a string of expletives. She knew him too damn well. No one should know him that well.

''Sorry it didn't work, but welcome back, friend,'' Robbie said with a wobbly grin.

And then it was Con who found himself retreating. It was either that, or haul her into his arms again. Only this time it wouldn't have been to teach her a lesson. If it ever had been.

Grabbing a pack of cigarettes out of the kitchen drawer, he headed for the door.

''Con?''

He turned around reluctantly. He needed some space.

''Don't touch me again,'' she said, her voice steadier than it had any right being. ''Not until you can do it without apologizing. Not until you can do it with more than just your body.''

Which meant never. ''I won't,'' he promised her. It was a promise he wasn't sure he could keep.

CHAPTER TEN

CON TOOK ONE MORE DRAG on his cigarette before crushing it in the car ashtray. Once he went inside, he wouldn't have another one. He hadn't smoked in the house in five days. Not since Friday when his son had arrived.

It had been three days since they'd seen Joey. It seemed like another lifetime. His gut had been eroding ever since.

Throwing his keys on the breakfast bar, Con headed straight for the fridge and a beer. God, he was tired. Tired to the bone. He'd been back to work for three days and already he was beat. The case he was working on was a local check counterfeiter, nothing big—not like Ramirez's organization had been. He'd be able to get the guy within the week. Too bad he didn't care.

The phone rang just as he was enjoying his first sip of beer.

"Randolph," he snapped into the receiver. If it was Robbie telling him she was going to be late again, he was going to wring her neck. She didn't have to avoid him, didn't have to worry that he was going to try to jump her bones again. That had to have been the all-time dumbest thing he'd ever done.

"Mr. Randolph? This is Karen Smith from social services."

"Yes?" Con said, bracing himself.

"There're a couple of things I need to discuss with you, sir," the woman said in a rush. "First, we've got a court date for the placement hearing. It's set for July thirtieth at ten. Is that all right for you?"

"I'll make sure it is," Con said, grabbing his pen and jotting down the date and time.

"Will your wife be attending with you?"

"Of course." He hoped Robbie was still around by then. Hell, he was beginning to hope she'd be around a lot longer than that. Though, after what he'd done Sunday night he wouldn't blame her if she'd already filed for divorce.

"Oh, good," Karen said, her relief apparent. Con heard what she wasn't saying. If Robbie wasn't there, they were all wasting their time.

"You said you had two things to discuss?" Con reminded the woman. There was something she didn't want to tell him. He could sense it.

"Yes, sir. It's just that...the baby's mother has come back into the picture."

Con felt the blood drain from his face. "Meaning?"

"Probably nothing," Karen was quick to assure him. "Except that she claims she's sorry and she's willing to do whatever is necessary to get custody of Joey."

"Is that possible?"

"Anything's possible," Karen said in her usual noncommittal way. "But personally I'm not sure she really means it. How well do you know Cecily Barnhardt, Mr. Randolph?"

He thought of the woman who'd sat beside him in the bar that night. He'd never even gotten a good look at her. "I don't know her at all," he said, though he suspected Karen knew that.

"She's very immature," Karen said calmly. "She appears to be looking for someone to take care of her, not someone to take care of. It's possible she heard you were back in the picture and has somehow assumed that if you want Joey, you'll take her in, too."

Con listened intently, drawing up a composite of Cecily Barnhardt in his mind, prepared to outthink the woman if necessary. "I'm married," he reminded Karen. At least for now.

"She may not know that," Karen replied. "In any case, the state is obligated to allow her time to prove herself a fit parent."

"How much time?"

"At least six months."

Con slammed down his beer. "The hearing's only three weeks away."

"That will be a placement hearing, Mr. Randolph, at which time you and your wife may be appointed as Joey's caregivers, but he'll remain a ward of the state until his custody is determined.''

Con digested that piece of information silently. Just more bad news he had to break to Robbie. It seemed as though that was all he ever did—bring her bad news. She'd been working like a madwoman for three days straight, and he knew it wasn't only because of him. She was missing the baby.

And so was he.

"I want to see him before then,'' he said. He was the boy's father. He had to have *some* rights.

"Certainly. Now that the DNA's back, you can have him every weekend if you like.''

The tension in Con's gut slowly disintegrated. "I like. How soon can we pick him up?''

"Friday, anytime after four. Betty Williams will have him ready.''

Robbie would be happy. Maybe even happy enough to forget what an ass he'd made of himself.

"Oh…Mr. Randolph? *If* you get placement, chances are good you'll get custody, too.''

Con hung up the phone, suddenly energized. He'd heard Karen's *if* loud and clear, but he'd always taken things one step at a time. And in just two days he'd see his son again. Two days until he and Robbie could put their own troubles aside and be a team once more.

But sometime during those two days he had to tell Robbie about Cecily Barnhardt's reentry into their lives. How in hell did a man tell his wife she might lose her baby to a woman her husband had slept with, when he'd never even slept with *her?*

CON DIDN'T GET AROUND to telling Robbie about Cecily before Friday. She'd been working late both Wednesday and Thursday, and he'd been up and gone in the mornings before she appeared. He'd left her a note on the breakfast bar telling her they would pick up Joey for the weekend, so she'd be sure to come home early on Friday. It was true they'd been avoiding each other, but he was banking on the baby to bring them back together again—and to be the buffer that would help him keep his hands off her.

But once they had Joey that afternoon, although he told her about the placement hearing, he was loath to mention Cecily. Their time with the boy was too limited. The hours spent with him were the best hours Con had ever had, and he couldn't bring himself to tarnish them with the messy details of their future— or his past.

Stan and Susan drove down from Sedona on Saturday, bearing far too many gifts. With Joey on her lap, Robbie unwrapped each one, holding it up in front of the baby as if he really understood what it was or that it was for him. Joey obliged her by staring at each of the various brightly colored toys. He even reached for a couple. A mouse that squeaked. And a plastic hourglass that was filled with water and brightly colored confetti.

Susan marveled at every move the baby made.

Even Stan got into the act, coaxing smile after smile out of the boy.

Con was content to watch, glad that Joey was getting the acceptance from this family he'd once craved so hopelessly for himself.

The weekend flew by. He and Robbie fell right back into parenting as if they'd been at it for years. They played with Joey; they shopped for more things they'd suddenly discovered they needed for him—a teething ring for one; they took turns feeding him and changing him.

Together they discovered new and amazing things about the little boy—the birthmark on his knee that was identical to Con's, the way he was starting to scoot himself around on his belly, the tooth they were sure was starting to come through. Together they pushed his stroller and answered proudly when people asked questions about him.

And together they drove him silently back to Gilbert on Sunday.

In one way this trip was made easier by the knowledge that they'd be getting Joey again in just five days. But for Con it was also more difficult. First, because as soon as the baby was gone, so would be the camaraderie he and Robbie had shared over the weekend.

And second, because he knew he had one more strike against him now, a strike Robbie knew nothing about. The boy's biological mother wanted him back.

THINGS WERE SHAPING UP. Now that he knew the woman was living with Randolph, he didn't have to watch the place so much. He still had to figure how he was going to get her out of there, but he had time. And ideas, too. He was having a real good time considering the ideas. He spent whole days just thinking about them. Yeah, maybe he'd take her at night. Maybe even when Randolph was home. Whatever way was going to make Randolph hurt the most.

He had the place to take her to. It was empty, but he'd slept there last night. Not too many crickets, but hot. He'd had to sleep naked.

He'd thought about making Randolph watch him do it to her before he took her away. Except he wasn't keen on hurting the woman. Not until he had to. Or on giving Randolph a chance to stop him. The bastard was good, and a lot bigger than he was. He had to be smart about this, had to get it right. He'd only get one chance. And his black belt in karate probably wouldn't faze a guy like Randolph.

No, he'd probably grab her when Randolph wasn't home. His percentages would be better that way. He'd just have to make certain that Randolph suffered afterward. A lot.

ROBBIE LEFT the TV station in time to make it home for dinner Monday night. She'd missed Con last week. But she'd needed the time away from him, time to recover from his assault on her senses, her heart.

She pulled onto Con's street, *her* street now, too,

waving at the teenager who was the neighborhood odd-job boy, out raking the gravel in the yard across the street.

Con had done her a favor, really. He'd been trying to shock her, make her not want him. But he'd also said something she'd needed to hear. It wasn't *her* his body was responding to, as she'd so desperately wanted to believe. It was his need for a woman. Any woman. He'd obviously been celibate for a while, and she had legs and breasts, both of which she'd shamelessly rubbed against him in the pool.

She pushed the button on the remote, and when the garage door opened, was disappointed to see that Con's car wasn't there. She pulled her truck into her side of the two-car garage, then lowered the door behind her.

She wasn't his type. She knew that. Had always known that. The women Con went for were her total opposite, helpless beauties every one of them. She'd seen enough of them come and go over the years. But she had something none of them had ever had, something far more precious than sex—Con's friendship.

She'd been content with that for twenty-five years. She couldn't let a little thing like this marriage change that.

Which was why she was glad he'd stopped when he had that night last week in the kitchen. As much as it had hurt, she knew it would have been a thousand times worse if they'd gotten as far as his bedroom or hers. By then it would have been too late to salvage anything. Not her heart. Not her marriage. And not their friendship.

She had spaghetti boiling in the pot when Con walked through the door half an hour later. She'd heard him pull in five minutes before and knew he'd been outside finishing his cigarette before he came in. She'd been very tempted to go out and join him. She hadn't had a cigarette in more than a week, and her nerves were jangling.

"I didn't expect you to be here," he said, throwing his keys on the breakfast bar next to one of Joey's pacifiers. There were clean bottles upside down on a towel on the counter, too.

Robbie shrugged, trying to remember how they used to act before they'd gotten married. "I was a little tired. Home sounded good."

He pulled a beer from the refrigerator, twisted off the cap and tossed it in the trash. "It's good to have you home," he said. She froze, her back to him, staring at the spaghetti as she blinked away a sudden rush of tears. He'd never said that to her before.

"Here—you want one?" he asked.

Robbie turned. He was holding out a beer.

Just like the old days. "Sure," she said, taking it from him, trying not to notice when his hand brushed hers. There was absolutely nothing seductive about the movement, but her body ignited, anyway. How in hell was she going to survive a lifetime of this?

"So what kind of blood and gore did you cover

today?'' he asked, getting out the tomato sauce for the spaghetti.

''I've been investigating a couple of nursing homes here in the valley,'' she said, ignoring her reactions to his nearness as best she could as they finished preparing the meal together.

He pulled a loaf of French bread from the freezer. ''Why?''

''They're owned by a group of doctors, all internists who specialize in geriatrics,'' she explained, frowning. ''We got this anonymous tip that the good doctors are convincing family members that patients need to be institutionalized before they really do.''

''Are they?''

Robbie shook her head, her short hair bobbing against her ears. ''That's just it, I don't know. I've visited the homes, Con, talked to many of the patients, and while some of them belong there without a doubt, there are others who seem perfectly capable of living at home. Yet the family members I've interviewed all insist they had no other choice.''

''You could be going for the wrong story,'' Con said, slicing the frozen bread. ''What you may have here are families who no longer want the burden of caring for their elderly.''

Robbie rinsed the lettuce for a salad. ''I don't think so, Con. One woman I spoke to was really broken up about having to institutionalize her husband. She spends every waking moment at the home with him. She'd do anything to have him back with her, but she's convinced he has to be there. So they're living the rest of their lives in a nursing home that's eating up all their savings."

Con frowned, quiet for so long that Robbie thought the discussion was over. She should have known better.

"I'd look for a younger family member," he finally said. "Maybe a son or daughter of the woman you just mentioned. Elderly people tend to be more dependent on their doctors, often taking a doctor's word as law. Possibly seeing symptoms they're told to see. They're also easier to convince. Someone younger might give you the insight you're missing."

Robbie nodded, knowing she should have come to him before now. She always had before. The man was an expert when it came to human motivation. She supposed it came from years of trying to please disapproving caregivers, of always putting himself in others' shoes. Or maybe he'd developed a sixth sense during his years as an agent. Lord knew it had helped save his life a time or two.

"Thanks, friend, I will," she said, suddenly feeling better than she had in days.

"Anytime."

Anytime. This was what she had from him, an open-ended twenty-four-hour-a-day invitation into his life. She had to let it be enough.

"ROBBIE, CAN I SEE YOU?" Rick Hastings called out into the newsroom late Tuesday afternoon.

She dropped what she was working on and walked into the producer's office.

"What's up?"

"I've been going over the tape of your interview with Blackwell this morning. Great stuff."

"Thanks." She'd even dressed up for the occasion and was still wearing her new pair of black jeans and a white blouse.

"I'd like you to do the piece live on the air."

Robbie's gaze flew to Rick's. He had to be kidding. He'd always told her she was one hell of an investigative reporter, but she didn't have the right look to actually report the stories she uncovered. Which was why her pieces were always dubbed. Someone else narrated her stuff on air, paraphrasing the questions she'd asked to correspond with clips of the subject's answers.

"We're running it tomorrow night at six. Report to makeup by five."

"You got it," she said, grinning. She was going to be on the air!

"Better make that four-thirty and stop off at wardrobe on your way."

"I'm not wearing any of those low-cut show-your-cleavage things Megan wears on the air."

"She wears them off the air, too," Rick reminded her. "That's just Megan. We'll find you something. Don't worry."

She wasn't worried. She was ecstatic, thrilled, excited as hell. She had to call Con.

"Oh, and Robbie?"

She looked back at the producer. "Yeah?"

"Joan and I are having a cookout on August third. It's a Saturday. You think you and Con can make it?"

"I'll check with him and get back to you," she said, still grinning.

It felt great to be included again. Life was good. Life was really good.

SHE'D CALLED CON first thing, and when she got home he was waiting there with a bottle of champagne.

"Congratulations," he said, toasting her as they sat together in the living room, the open bottle on the coffee table. Still in her black jeans and white blouse, Robbie was sitting on the floor, leaning against the couch. Con had changed out of his suit to shorts and a cotton shirt and was lounging on the other end of the sofa. "Though I still say your reporting isn't grunt work. You have a real talent for getting to the truth."

"Thanks," she said, sipping her champagne. "You know, I really never thought this day would come."

"Why not? You wanted it."

She looked over at him. "What's that supposed to mean?"

"You always get what you want. Always have."

She burst out laughing. "I do not."

It was funny someone could know you for so long and still have an entirely different perception of you than you had of yourself. A false perception. She'd never had the one thing she'd always wanted most.

Him.

"What about that time you wanted to play football?"

"I was good enough to be on that team, Con. And I was a cop's kid. The team was for cop's kids. There was no reason I shouldn't have played."

His lips curved into the half grin she loved. "You were the only girl on the team, Rob."

So she'd caused a bit of ruckus, but she'd done the team and her father proud. "Yeah, well, you didn't seem to find anything wrong with it back then. If I remember correctly, you were the one who taught me to play in the first place."

They sipped silently for a couple of minutes. Her memories of those days had to be a whole lot happier than Con's.

"What about that Jeep you just had to have for your sixteenth birthday?" he asked.

"I worked hard for that Jeep, Con. I paid my dad back every cent, plus paid for insurance and gas."

He frowned. "I never said you didn't work hard. You've always worked hard. Which is why you always get what you want."

She smiled sadly into her champagne.

Not always.

CON MADE SURE he was home by six the next evening. He'd been looking forward to Robbie's debut all day. He was proud of her.

She'd called him that afternoon to tell him that her piece on Blackwell was being picked up by stations all over the country. He wasn't surprised. He'd always known she'd make it big. If not in news reporting, then doing something else. She was just one of those people.

After pulling a beer out of the fridge, he wandered into the bedroom and flipped on the television set while he stripped off his suit and tie. The temperature had been well over a hundred all week. He'd done nothing but sweat the whole time.

A swim sounded good. A nice cool swim. Right after the news.

He tossed his clothes on the end of his bed, which was huge and took up most of the room. He'd had to have the bed specially made so he could sleep without his feet hanging over the end.

He heard the news come on, listened to Megan Brandt do the headlines. Padding in from the bathroom naked, he sat down on the end of the bed.

"We've all been reading his comics for years..." He heard Robbie's voice. He even made out the first few words she said. But the rest was lost on him as he sat and stared at his television set. Who was this woman? He hardly recognized her.

Her hair, normally flat against her head, was fluffed up like a fashion model's. She was wearing a dress, a navy thing that hugged her waist and ended several inches above her knees, exposing far more of her miles of legs than he was comfortable with. And she had makeup on, which widened her eyes and gave her lips a fuller "come kiss me" look.

How in hell was he supposed to convince himself she was still just his buddy when she looked like that?

He felt his body tighten as he continued to stare at the woman standing before him, who sounded every bit as confident as she looked.

Shit. He wanted her. Still.

"YOU WERE RIGHT," Robbie told Con later that evening. They were sitting in the kitchen, sharing a beer.

"Right about what?" He seemed awfully interested in his fingernails.

"Reporting isn't grunt work. It's what I love."

Con looked up. "Being on air wasn't all you thought it was?"

"Nope." She'd learned something about herself tonight. Something she'd thought she already knew, but apparently she'd needed the reminder. She was who she was. She couldn't change that.

She'd thought that if she looked like Megan Brandt she might be able to stir Con's blood. But she'd felt like an idiot. If Con didn't want her for herself, then so be it.

"I'm going to stick to reporting," she said, taking the beer from him. The bottle was still warm from his lips.

"Have you told Rick?"

"Uh-huh."

"And?"

She shrugged. "He said I was great at both. The choice is mine."

"Good."

She glanced up, surprised at the emphatic tone in his voice.

"You're too damn good at what you do to be a puppet, saying only what other people tell you to say."

Warmth flooded her. "Newscasters are more than that," she said, laughing to cover her sudden flare of desire for him.

Con grunted and finished off their beer.

"You still working on that nursing-home story?" he asked, and got up to throw away the empty bottle.

Robbie got to her feet, too. "Tomorrow I have an appointment with the daughter of the patient I told you about. She's having her father examined by another doctor."

Con nodded. He didn't seem surprised by her about-face. Hell, he'd probably known all along it wouldn't take much for her to figure out where she belonged. He knew her that well.

"Rick's having a party on August third," she told him. "It's a Saturday. You wanna go?"

"Can Joey come along?"

She'd already asked that question herself. "Yep. It's for families."

"It's not a pool party, is it?" he asked, his back to her as he rinsed a couple of glasses in the sink.

She'd checked that out, too. Neither of them needed that kind of temptation again. "Nope."

"Sure, we can go."

Robbie moved to the door. "I'll tell Rick tomorrow," she said. "Good night."

"Night."

"Rob?" She was halfway down the hall when he called her back.

She stuck her head around the corner. "Yeah?"

"I was proud of you tonight."

As HE HEADED into work the next morning, Con realized he'd better tell Robbie about Cecily tonight, before they got Joey again for the weekend. He'd been putting off telling her because he hadn't wanted to spoil the truce they seemed to have reached last weekend. He'd also been preoccupied all week following the paper trail that would nail his local check counterfeiter.

Several hours later he was standing at the door of the apartment he'd traced his counterfeiter to, his backup in the apartment building next door. The folder beneath his arm was loaded with photocopies of enough evidence to put Tommy Boyer away for years.

Unless the guy wanted to help Con out by fingering his supplier. Because Con had discovered something interesting the day before. The paper Tommy Boyer was using to print his checks had the same pattern of red squares under ultraviolet light that several of the banks in the valley were using as a means of protection against check fraud. Which meant if a bank teller ran Boyer's checks under an ultraviolet light to see if the checks were valid, he or she would see the red squares and assume they were.

He'd only seen that paper fall into illegal hands once before. Nick Ramirez's. And Con had been certain he'd cleared out every contact in Ramirez's organization. He'd made it his personal project.

Holding his folder, which also contained an arrest warrant, in one hand, Con knocked on apartment number 2006. Boyer would be home. He liked to watch the cooking show that was on cable every day at noon.

"Just a minute," the young man called irritably through the door. Con heard some shuffling, as if something was being hurriedly put away, and then the door was cracked open.

"Yeah? Whaddaya want?" Tommy Boyer's pimply nose was about all Con could see.

"I have a deal. Martin sent me," Con said, playing a hunch and naming Ramirez's personal shopkeeper. Whatever Ramirez needed, Martin had a contact who could supply it, whether it be Uzis or marked paper. Martin was doing twenty years in the federal penitentiary, compliments of Con, but apparently he still had someone on the outside Con didn't know about. Someone not as smart as Martin. Someone who'd made the mistake of doing business with a small-time crook like Tommy Boyer.

"You alone?" Boyer's voice had dropped to a near whisper.

"Yeah," Con said, lowering his voice, also. If clandestine was what Boyer expected, then clandestine was what Con would give him. He didn't want to alarm him by not playing the game the right way.

Boyer opened his door just enough to let Con inside, then shut the door quickly.

The young man's apartment looked like a computer nerd's dream. Con surveyed the living room, noticing the top-of-the-line equipment, desktop computer, color laser printer, even a scanner.

"Wow, man, ain't you hot in that suit?" Boyer said. "it's 120 degrees out there."

"No," Con said, staring at the young man, who was wearing glasses and a pair of boxer shorts. Period.

"You know Martin?" Boyer asked. The kid was still too cocky with his recent successes to be intimidated by Con's size. But that would come.

"You could say that."

"What kinda deal you got?"

Con stepped closer to him. The young man's glasses slid down his nose.

So he wasn't as cool as he wanted Con to think. Con relaxed. This was going to be a piece of cake. "It depends. How do you feel about prison?"

Boyer's hands started to shake. "Why?" He

backed away. Behind him was an easy chair and an end table with a couple of drawers.

As Con started to reach into his inside jacket pocket for his FBI badge, Boyer sprung for the top drawer of the end table and came up with a pistol so fast he had to have practiced the maneuver. A lot.

Con had practice, too. He grabbed Boyer's arm. "Hold it right there," he said, his iron grip applying pressure in just the right spot to force Boyer to drop the gun. Then he picked it up, intending to empty it of bullets.

"You're a little jumpy there, aren't you, boy?" he asked, his voice calm, easy.

"It ain't even loaded," Boyer said, his hands still shaking. "What was you goin' for in your pocket just then?"

"Cigarettes." Con verified that the gun wasn't loaded, dropped it back on the table and pulled out his cigarettes. "You want one?"

"Lemme see 'em."

Con held the pack up. Anything to get the kid to cooperate. "See? Just cigarettes," Con said, pulling one from the pack with his lips and lighting it. "Got an ashtray?" he asked, looking around.

He knew exactly where Tommy's ashtray was. Next to his desktop computer, with a half-smoked joint lying in it.

Tommy grabbed the ashtray. The joint was missing when he held it out to Con.

"You know, Martin gets nervous doing business

with hotheads," Con said conversationally, leaning back against Boyer's dinette table. "I don't like it much, either."

"I didn't mean nothin'," Boyer said, then his tone turned pleading. "You ain't gonna tell him, are you?"

With his cigarette hanging from his mouth, Con reached into his jacket a second time.

"I'm with the FBI," he said, flipping out his badge.

He'd never seen the blood drain from someone's face so quickly. Tommy Boyer turned white and then a sickly green. "I didn't want to do it, man. They made me," he whined.

"Who are 'they'?" Con asked. This was going to be easier than easy.

Boyer's gaze darted around the room. "I don't know. They just have me collect information over the Internet."

He was lying. Con wasn't sure why.

"How do you contact them?"

"Someone comes here. I never know who or when." The words were coming too quickly, like they'd been practiced as many times as pulling the gun had been.

"Those old guys in prison, they've been locked up so long they're really hungry for fresh young guys like you, you know that?" Con asked. He wanted the truth. He wanted to know whether Martin and Ramirez were back in business. Or *still* in business.

Boyer started to tremble. "Really, man, I don't do nothin' but surf the Net."

Con had no idea what the kid was talking about. He had Boyer on check counterfeiting. Small-time sloppy check fraud. On professional paper. He stared silently at the young man.

"You said something about a deal. Was that just to get in here?" Boyer blurted.

Con's eyes narrowed through his cigarette smoke. "No."

"Let's hear it."

"I want Martin."

Con saw relief flash across the kid's face at the same time as he heard a key in the door behind him. He wondered if maybe he should have brought someone inside with him, after all.

Feeling for the gun in his shoulder holster with the side of his arm, he gauged the distance between Boyer and the door.

"Hi, baby, I'm back," a woman called, coming inside. She didn't see Con right away. But the man right behind her did. He had his gun out and trained on a spot between Con's eyes as quickly as Con had drawn his own gun.

Con held his weapon steady, waiting for someone to move, swearing under his breath. The kid hadn't had a single visitor all week. Suddenly he had a damn houseful. And Con had some quick thinking to do, a new game to play.

Three against one.

WORD CAME OVER the police radio at the television station that an FBI agent was trapped inside an apartment in Phoenix with three suspects, at least one of them armed. The agent's partner was set up in an apartment facing it, watching everything through an unadorned window.

Rick Hastings heard the news first. And immediately sent George Nelson out to cover the unfolding drama. "Take Darrin with you," he yelled, naming the station's star photographer.

"I'm going along," Robbie said, her voice full of steel.

"No." Rick didn't even look her way.

"Yes, Rick. I'm going," she insisted. Her heart was pounding so hard she could hardly breathe, but she had to go. She knew most of the local agents.

"No." Rick still didn't look up from the filing cabinet he was thumbing through.

"I'll see you tomorrow," she said, grabbing her things, hoping to catch a ride with George and Darrin.

"It's Con, Robbie."

Rick's words stopped her in her tracks.

HE WAS GROCERY SHOPPING, figuring out which sugared cereal was cheapest, when the music being piped over the loudspeaker was suddenly interrupted. "FBI Special Agent Connor Randolph is inside a west Phoenix apartment believed to be occupied by at least one member of the Nick Ramirez organization. Ramirez's professional crime organization was broken up by Randolph's team almost two years ago. Randolph's partner on the investigation, FBI Agent Steve Corrinth, reports that two more individuals entered the apartment just moments ago. It is believed that at least one of the individuals is armed, though as of this report no shots have been fired. Agents have been called in and are surrounding the building...."

Damn! He let loose a string of expletives that would have made his mama cringe, left his half-full cart in the cereal aisle and walked out of the store. He had to get to a television. Find out what was happening.

They *couldn't* have him. They didn't deserve to have him. *He* was going to get Randolph. He was going to squeeze every last bit of anguish he could out of the bastard. The man didn't deserve a quick death. *He* was going to kill him slowly.

His plans were well under way. He was in the process of making the place real nice. He'd brought his mattress from home and bought some new sheets at the flea market. He was stocking up on food and soap and other stuff a woman might want or need. He'd bought some coffee, though he couldn't stand the stuff. She was going to be real comfortable. He'd even sprayed the place so the crickets wouldn't bug her. She wasn't going to suffer while he kept her. She'd never done anything to him. Randolph was the one who'd suffer, bit by excruciating bit. And at the end, of course, he'd have to kill her, too. To make it right.

But that was a long way off. First he was going to love telling Randolph he was balling his woman. He was making lists of all the things he was going to let Randolph think he was doing to the babe. Things he hadn't even known a guy *could* do till he started his research. He'd be ready by the end of the month. Ready to teach Randolph all he'd learned.

Provided, of course, they didn't kill Randolph first. Rage filled his soul as he thought about losing this chance. They couldn't kill him. Randolph was *his*.

CHAPTER ELEVEN

SITTING IN RICK'S OFFICE, a paper cup filled with brandy held between shaking hands, Robbie heard it all. Her boss was there, his wife, Joan, too, and everyone else not otherwise occupied at the station. She sipped the brandy slowly as she waited for news over the police radio, getting only a scrap of information at a time. She heard descriptions of the suspects, which agents were on the scene or close by. She heard Con's credentials.

She held herself together until reports came that a shot had been fired.

And then her whole body started to shake. All she could think about was Con lying in a pool of blood. The life seeping out of him.

She was hardly aware when Joan took her hand. If Con was dead, so was she. Con. Dead.

Stop it! she cried silently. Con was the best there was. He always got his man, even if there were three of them.

A second shot was reported and Robbie thought about Joey. He needed Con. He deserved to know him. To learn from him. To be loved by him. Huge tears rolled slowly down her cheeks.

Letting go of Joan's hand and putting down the cup of brandy, Robbie wrapped her arms around her middle, holding on for all she was worth. She just had to wait a little longer. Shots had been fired. The other agents would have moved in. Soon everyone would know what was happening. Soon they'd tell her Con was all right. She just had to hold on.

"NO! I'M NOT DOING TIME for murder!" Boyer yelled, interrupting the threats that had been passing back and forth between Con and Perez. Both men still had their guns trained on each other.

"Shut up, kid," Perez growled. The woman moved across the room, hovering by the easy chair and end table.

Con stood frozen, waiting for his moment. Then Boyer, eyes wild, lunged at Perez. "No, I didn't agree to any murder!"

He grabbed at the arm holding the gun, and Con made his move. He dived for Perez, grabbing the man's gun hand in a viselike grip above their heads as they started to fall. Con's gun dropped to the floor beneath them. Perez's gun went off.

Screaming, Boyer backed away. Con was vaguely aware of the kid sinking to the floor by the easy chair, mumbling incoherently. One down.

Con rolled with Perez, turning to take the knee intended for his groin in the thigh, instead, still holding Perez's gun hand above their heads, applying pressure for all he was worth. He'd lost track of the woman.

The gun went off a second time, the acrid smell filling the air.

Con landed a couple of good blows, one with his elbow, one with his fist. Perez wasn't as big as he was, but he was younger, and strong as an ox.

Rolling back on top, Con slammed the other man's arm to the floor. Perez still didn't lose the gun. Con pulled him up, then smashed him back to the floor. Perez doubled back with a fist to Con's nose and right eye.

"Hold it right there." Both men froze as the woman's voice came from right beside Con's head. She was holding a gun about a foot from Con's temple.

"Oh, God, no. He's FBI," he heard Boyer whimper. "You know what happens to you if you kill an FBI agent?"

"He's the scum who put your father behind bars," Perez said, relaxing his grip on his gun slightly as he saw the battle about to end in his favor. Con slammed Perez's hand against the floor one more time, knocking the gun loose—just as the gun in the woman's hand clicked quietly.

Boyer's gun.

Con flipped Perez over onto his stomach before the other man knew what was happening, then grabbed his own gun from the floor just as the door burst open to half a dozen FBI agents.

He got to his feet, wiped the blood from his nose, straightened his jacket and walked out of the apartment, leaving someone else to mop up—for now.

The world was full of Boyers and Perezes, Martins and Ramirezes. They just kept coming at him. And he just kept nailing them.

He found it one of life's cruel ironies that the only thing he was really good at was something he'd grown to hate.

ROBBIE WAS STILL trembling inside and out as she gripped the steering wheel, heading home after word had come that it was all over. Con was all right. Logically she knew that. He had a couple of bruises, that was all. He'd be on his way home soon.

But until she saw him, until she felt his warm body with her own two hands, her heart was afraid to believe. She'd almost lost Con today. Dear God, she'd almost lost him.

And once she'd assured herself that he was really all right, she was going to kill him for putting her through this hell.

CON WAS BEAT when he pulled into his driveway. His nose still throbbed and his muscles were going to be sore as hell in the morning.

But Ramirez was out of business again. Before Con had even known the guy was back up and running.

What had started out as a small-time arrest had turned into something with international ramifications. He'd gone after Tommy Boyer, curious about the small-time check counterfeiter's paper supplier, unaware that the kid was Martin's illegitimate son.

Boyer had been working as Martin's Internet connection for the rebuilding of Ramirez's organization ever since Martin and Ramirez had gone to the slammer. Boyer had been passing information gleaned from hacking to Martin's girlfriend, who then passed it on to Martin during her weekly visits with him at the penitentiary.

But Martin had made a critical mistake when he'd trusted the son he'd run out on a decade before. A two-bit punk, Tommy Boyer had thought he was smarter than his father. He'd been running his own little check-counterfeiting business on the side with no one the wiser, using Martin's suppliers.

Which is how Con had become suspicious that Ramirez was back in business and made the decision to go after Boyer himself. Going in alone had proved more dangerous, but it had been the surest way to enlist Boyer's trust—to ultimately get Ramirez.

And no one had died, at least not yet. He didn't hold out much hope for Tommy Boyer. If the punk lived long enough to make it to prison, Ramirez would get him there. The stupid greedy kid had just handed the feds an entire organization.

Of course it hadn't all been Boyer's doing. Some of it had been pure luck. If Martin hadn't been on to his son, if he hadn't sent his hit man to take out Boyer at the exact moment Con was there, Con might not have put it all together so fast. But he'd recognized Perez. He'd just been a little surprised to see him alive, since the guy had been reportedly killed in a prison riot earlier in the summer.

Robbie's car was in the garage when he pulled in. Tired as he was, he was glad to see it there.

She was sitting at the breakfast bar when he entered the kitchen, an open pack of his cigarettes on the counter. Judging by the ashtray in front of her, she'd smoked at least half the pack.

His gaze went to her face.

Her cheeks were devoid of color. Her eyes were red-rimmed, as if she'd been crying. And they were wary.

"Hi," he said, still standing there staring at her. He didn't know what else to do.

"Hi."

"You have dinner yet?"

She shook her head. "I've been waiting for you."

His exhaustion lifted a little. It was still a novel experience coming home from a hard day to find someone waiting for him. Anyone waiting. But especially Robbie. "You heard?" he said.

He hadn't needed to ask. It was obvious she'd been worried as hell. It was written all over her face. "Yeah. I was at the station when it came in over the radio."

Con walked toward her, dropping his keys on the counter, then lighting himself a cigarette when she continued to watch him. What did she want from him?

"Boyer was Martin's illegitimate son," he said.

She nodded, but didn't seem to want to hear any more. "How's your eye?"

The intensity of her gaze had him on his guard. Where was his hotshot reporter? The one who fired questions faster than he could answer them?

"Sore."

"You're gonna have quite a shiner by morning."

Con nodded, still watching her. She seemed so calm sitting there, but he sensed something roiling under the surface. He just couldn't fathom what it was.

She sat there for another moment and then ground out her cigarette and stood up. "Dammit, Con!" she yelled, all traces of calm gone. "Why in hell did you go in there alone? You have a family now! People who need you! How dare you do that to Joey?"

Her words took Con totally by surprise. His life, or death, had never mattered before. "It was going to be a piece of cake," he said.

"It doesn't matter what it was going to be! What matters is what was. When they said shots were fired, I thought you'd been killed, Con!"

There were tears in her voice.

"My job's dangerous. You've always known that."

"But you could have lessened the danger just by having someone else with you."

"We had a better shot of getting Boyer to talk if I went in alone."

"And your life was worth getting some rotten punk to talk? Damn you! Damn you to hell!"

In that second their whole relationship changed. Robbie had always cared about him, just as he'd cared about her—but without expectations, without investing more than they could afford to lose.

But Robbie was acting as if she'd almost lost something that would have mattered.

Reacting purely on instinct, he pulled her into his arms, holding her against his chest. "I'm sorry, Rob."

She shuddered, squeezing him tightly. "It was stupid, Con. Stupid to go in there alone. Joey needs you," she said, her words muffled against him.

"I'm sorry," he said again. He'd never had anyone who cared before, never had anyone to consider when he went to work. "I'll send someone else next time."

And he would, if he had any choice at all. Because it mattered. For the first time in his life *he* mattered to someone.

She looked up at him, her grin a little wobbly. "It's just a good thing you made it back okay. I didn't want to have to kill you for screwing up."

She was better.

He should let her go. He smiled at her, instead.

"He really got you good," she said, running her fingers softly along the tender skin beneath his right eye.

"I got him better."

"I'm sure you did."

They continued to gaze deeply into each other's eyes, assessing, wondering about things that hadn't been said. And slowly Robbie's eyes took on a light he'd never seen in them before. Determined, hungry and all woman.

"I'm sure you did," she said again softly. Then, hooking her hand around his neck, she pulled him gently down until his lips met hers.

There was passion in her kiss, kindling an answering passion in him, but there was something else, something Con craved even more. He followed her lead, opening his mouth to explore her sweetness.

The instant their tongues met, sweetness and whatever else he'd been seeking was forgotten. Everything was forgotten but the flames spreading through his body. He'd been living with her for weeks, listening to her shower and dress, undress and shower, climb into bed. He could no longer pretend he didn't want her with every fiber of his being.

His need drove him, deepening the kiss as his body hardened against hers.

His hands spread across her back, spanning her waist. His wife's waist.

She whimpered, but when he lifted his head she pulled it right back down, thrusting her tongue against his again. She wasn't letting him go.

His fingers slid lower, over the curves of her hips, down to cup her bottom. He was afraid he was going to explode. She was glorious. So much a woman. Firing him to the point of insanity.

So damn bold.

So Robbie.

Con jerked away from her, holding his hands up as if they didn't belong to him, as if he wasn't responsible for what they'd done. Where they'd been.

"Hell," he swore, turning away. He leaned one hand on the breakfast bar, studying the pattern in the ceramic tiles.

He'd made a promise. And he'd made it for a damn good reason. Because as badly as he wanted her, he couldn't have her. He couldn't reduce what they'd spent most of their lives building to a few minutes of sex.

Because that was all it would be. All it could ever be with him. A few minutes of sex.

But it was equally obvious that they weren't going to be able to continue on as they were. For whatever reason, his damn libido had decided to notice Robbie after all these years. The simple truth was, he wanted her so badly he couldn't trust himself to stay away from her.

"We're going to have to end this marriage," he said, thinking out loud. It was the only solution. And he'd get used to the idea. He wouldn't hate it so much once he'd had some sleep. He was just worn-out.

Not saying a word, she stared at him, her eyes filled with pain. A raw naked pain he'd never seen there before. *Damn.* It might already be too late. He might already have lost her.

"I'll see to it in the morning," he said, brushing past her. He was in for one helluva long night.

"What about Joey?"

Her question stopped him. He turned around and stared at her, too tired to come up with any more answers, to make sense of anything. Could he continue to use Robbie to get his son? Was he really going to get his man, his boy, rather, at any cost?

"We can't lose him, Con. Not when we're this close."

"The marriage will have to end, Robbie," he said. There was no way he could last a lifetime of living with her and not touching her. And after he'd had her, he'd have killed the one good thing he'd ever had going for him.

She nodded, swallowing back tears. "But after we get Joey."

If they got Joey. He needed to tell her about Cecily, too, about the newest strike against him, but right now he was just too damned tired.

"The court date's in less than two weeks," she said when he remained silent.

Surely he could keep his fly done up for two more weeks. "Fine."

She bowed her head, and as much as he wanted to, Con couldn't just walk away from her.

"I'm sorry," he said.

"Don't be." Her head shot up. "I don't blame you, Con. You can't help the way you feel any more than I can help what I am."

He frowned at the strange tone in her voice.

"What you are?"

"Too aggressive, bossy. It's a turnoff. I understand."

"Is that what you think?"

"It's what I know," Robbie said. She'd blown it. And the only way she could see to salvage anything between them was just to get the problem out in the open. Maybe if they could talk about it, they could put it behind them. Maybe, someday, they could be friends again.

"You're nuts." Con was scowling at her, his face lined with fatigue.

"Let's just call it like it is and be done with it, Con. Twenty-five years of friendship allows that, at least, doesn't it?"

"I don't know," he said, suddenly wary.

"Look. This isn't the first time this has happened to me and it's probably not going to be the last. Why do you think I'm thirty-three years old and still not married?"

"You're married."

Robbie knew he was trying to spare her feelings, but he was only making things worse. She waved her hand dismissively. "I know all about it, Con. I've been told a number of times that if I'd only let a man be the man, I'd have a lot more luck getting one. My father warned me about my aggressive behavior the day I told him you and I were getting married. And I even overheard the guys at work talking about it."

"Talking about what?"

Robbie wanted to curl up and die, but she had to get through this. She'd never forgive herself if she couldn't at least salvage a friendship with Con.

"How going to bed with me would be nothing but a turnoff," she replied quickly, trying to sound as if she didn't care. "And the thing is, I understand. I really do. I'm aggressive. I take control. I'm bossy, even in bed. I like to be on top," she confessed, her voice breaking in spite of her attempts to control it.

"What?"

"It's okay, Con, really. I am who I am. I'm not willing to change that. So you see, the choice really is mine."

"There's nothing wrong with being on top," he said, hauling her against him.

Robbie fought him for all she was worth, pushing against his iron grasp. She didn't want him to touch her. Not now. Not like this. Not in pity.

"You got it wrong, babe, so damn wrong," he said, controlling her with very little effort.

"It's OK, Con. You don't have to lie to me," she said, going still in his arms. But she didn't look at him. She couldn't. She didn't trust herself not to settle for whatever crumbs he might throw her.

"I wish I *was* lying," he said harshly, grabbing her hand and putting it against his groin. "You feel that? That's what you do to me. And I don't know where you learned about sex, babe, but that isn't what I'd call a turnoff."

Robbie's hand cupped him. She shouldn't, she was making a huge mistake, but she couldn't stop herself. She had to feel him. Just once.

"It's been a while since you've had a woman," she said, reminding herself of the fact even while she ran her hand along the length of him. Oh, Lord, he was marvelous.

He didn't stop her. "It's you, Rob. All you."

She dropped her hand. "Maybe. I doubt it."

"Tell my body that," he said derisively.

Something in his tone, in the desperate look in his eyes, got through to her. But still, she couldn't quite believe. "It's only until I do something that turns you off."

"I don't think there's anything you *could* do to turn me off," he said. "And God help me, I don't think there's any way I can resist, either. I gotta take you to bed, Rob. Now."

She wished he sounded happier about the prospect, but she was suddenly too needy to care. She could have lost him today. Her body, her heart, was starved for him. She couldn't pull away when he grabbed her hand and hauled her down the hall to his bedroom.

CON WASN'T a gentle lover. He wasn't a slow one, either. He fell with her to the bed immediately, his mouth covering hers even before she caught her breath. He rolled on top of her, his arms on either side of her head as he plundered her mouth, demanding everything she had.

His urgency fueled her, allowing her to be as wild with her passion as her nature demanded. Crazy with her unexpected freedom, she ran her hands all over him, touching him as she'd been dying to do for years. His body was rock solid. Everywhere. *He* was everywhere.

His huge hands spanned her body, making her feel fragile for the first time in her life. Fragile in a good way. A precious way.

He touched her face, her shoulders, her back, her buttocks again, pulling her against him, holding her right where she wanted to be. And then his hands were under her T-shirt, under her bra, cupping her breasts.

Robbie would gladly have died right then and there so perfect was the moment.

Except that Con had other plans.

He yanked her shorts down over her hips, pulled his slacks only as far as his thighs and positioned himself above her.

"You're a little hampered, there," Robbie said with a wobbly smile. She couldn't believe how nervous she was all of a sudden, or how glad that he wanted her this much. "Why not let me take it from here?"

She rolled over and straddled him, sitting above his rigid length. Con completed their union with one hard thrust.

And then brought her to an incredible climax. As she exploded around him, Robbie knew her life was never going to be the same again. There'd be no going back. No reclaiming what was hers. She'd just given herself utterly to him.

"God, you're good," Con said, his voice rough as he thrust again. His eyes were closed, his face a study of concentration.

"So good," he said, shuddering when he finally poured himself into her.

Robbie's heart soared as she watched him, as she went with him to paradise.

But the journey was far too short. When Con opened his eyes there was no love there, no warmth. Just the look of a satisfied male. The same impersonal look he might have given a stranger he'd happened to have sex with.

He rolled away almost immediately, then stood to yank his pants back up and fasten them. He still had his jacket on, his tie only slightly askew.

"I hope I convinced you," he said before he turned and left the room. A moment later she heard him leave the house.

CHAPTER TWELVE

THE PHONE WOKE Robbie from a troubled sleep early
the next morning. She didn't even know Con was in
the house until she heard him answer it. He hadn't
yet returned home when she'd finally gone to bed
sometime after three o'clock in the morning.

She hated herself for the relief she felt.

Con was nothing to her, she reminded herself.
Twenty years of infatuation was over. Dead.

Though the night she had just spent had been the
worst in her life, in a way she was grateful to Con.
In less than half an hour, he'd cured her of a lifelong
obsession. Because as good as her time in his arms
had been, it wasn't anything she wanted to repeat.
She'd rather live the rest of her life celibate than let
Con touch her again under those terms.

She'd made love to him. She'd given him everything, her passion, her heart, her innermost being.
She'd trusted him.

He'd had sex.

She'd showered twice after he'd gone, but she
hadn't been able to erase the feel of him from her
body.

"Robbie?" he called from just outside her door.

She pulled the covers up over her breasts, smoothing down the hair that she was sure was sticking up all over her head. ''Yeah?''

She didn't want him to see her, didn't want to see *him*. She could hardly bear her memories of last night.

He opened the door, but she could have been a cleaner mopping the floor for all the notice he took of her.

''That was Karen Smith. The hearing's been moved up to this Monday at nine.''

Monday at nine? She sat up. Something far more important than the last twenty-four hours was suddenly at stake. Joey. Did it have to be so soon? Were they ready? ''Do we still get him today?'' she asked.

He nodded. ''I'm picking him up at four. Meet me here at three if you want to go along.''

''Sure.'' Was this stranger the same man who'd swept her off to bed less than twelve hours before? Was he just going to pretend it had never happened?

''We still have to take him back on Sunday,'' he said. She watched him standing in her doorway and had a sudden vision of how he'd looked as she climbed astride him the night before.

Licking dry lips, she said, ''I figured. But we get him back right away again Monday morning if the judge gives us placement, right?''

Con nodded. He hesitated as if there was more he wanted to say, and she held her breath. Could he somehow take away the terrible heartache he'd left when he'd walked out on her last night?

Could he explain why he'd treated her like a whore?

"See you at three," he said, and left.

Damn him to hell for not loving me.

Robbie damned the foolish tears that fell, too, as she rolled over and buried her face in the pillow.

SHE COULDN'T HATE HIM any more than he hated himself. But that didn't stop his gut from clenching, didn't stop him from hurting, when she avoided his touch as he opened the car door for her that afternoon. Nor did he hurt any less when she couldn't look at him.

He slammed the door after her, knowing he was getting what he deserved. He'd screwed her. And by doing so, he'd screwed them both. Right out of the best friendship, the only friendship, he'd ever had. Stan had been right—that simply by being with him Robbie was bound to be hurt sooner or later. And there wasn't a damn thing he could do about it.

Except be glad she hated him. She wasn't going to have any trouble getting on with her life once Joey's future had been decided. Con just wasn't so sure what he'd have left of his own.

THE BOY RECOGNIZED HIM. Standing just behind Robbie at the door of Joey's foster home, Con could hardly believe it when the kid smiled right at him and held out his arms. He scooped the boy up, holding him close to his heart. He didn't deserve this. He hadn't asked for this chance, had never intended to saddle a kid with a father like him or bring a kid into a world like his, but it had happened, anyway. And for once in his life he was going to make himself proud. He was going to be there for his kid, make Joey's life a good one.

God help the judge, the system, that tried to tell him he couldn't raise his son.

"How's our little boy?" Robbie crooned to the baby, tickling his toes, his chubby little legs where they peeked out of the one-piece outfit he was wearing.

Her eyes met Con's briefly, the first time they'd done so that day. They were wary, but they didn't scald him. The knot in Con's chest loosened just a little. He'd hurt her, but she was going to be OK.

"Let's go home," he said.

"You'll have him back by six on Sunday?" Betty Williams asked, reminding them that they weren't alone.

"Yeah," Con said, turning with his son in his arms to head back to the car.

"Have a good weekend," Con heard the woman call behind him. With Joey with them, they just might.

And maybe, if they got the boy again on Monday, he and Robbie could manage to have a good rest of their lives, too. Maybe they could live together, raise their son and never touch each other again.

Yeah, sure, Con thought derisively. Because get-

ting Joey on Monday was a bigger "if" than he cared
to contemplate at the moment, and keeping his hands
off Robbie wasn't something he trusted himself to do,
either. He'd never wanted a woman so much after
he'd already had her. He wanted her again and again.
On top. Underneath. And standing straight up.

But he wasn't going to lay a finger on her. He was
going to keep his hands to himself until he could get
her safely out of his life. Or at least out of his house.
Because if he didn't, he'd keep using her until she
was all used up. That was just the kind of guy he was.

THE WEEKEND was excruciating. Filled with the
promise of dreams already lost. With the threat of
broken futures. And at the same time, it was strangely
happy. An interlude of right in a world of wrong.

Robbie suddenly understood how couples in unhappy marriages stayed together for years because of
the children. Joey was a buffer. The need to lavish
attention on him kept them from having to discuss
anything personal. He was also the cement binding
them together. In the battle of life it was the three of
them against the world.

And with the responsibility of the baby drawing
them closer, Robbie slowly started to heal. Not because she could ever forget the devastatingly impersonal way Con had had sex with her, but because all
weekend long, in so many little ways, she could feel
his caring, his respect.

He respected her opinion, even seeking it out on a

number of occasions. He insisted on holding a fussy Joey so she could eat Friday night's meat loaf while it was still hot. He brought a cup of coffee in to her Saturday morning when the baby woke her just after dawn for his bottle.

She could almost convince herself that they could still be a family just as they'd planned. Con hadn't said any more about ending the marriage. And in spite of everything, Robbie didn't want to end it, either. She loved Con. Had always loved him. And she loved his son. She wanted to raise Joey, be the one he ran to when he scraped his knee, the one he took for granted during adolescence. The one he thanked on national television when he grew up to be famous.

She even tried to convince herself that she'd be able to handle it when Con took other women to his bed in the coming years. After all, she now knew firsthand what they were getting. Or more importantly, what they weren't getting. She just had to not think about the incredible moments in Con's arms and concentrate on the seconds it took him to walk out on her afterward.

Or so she kept telling herself.

The low point of the weekend came during a visit from Susan and Stan on Sunday. Aware of the court date looming just a day away, Robbie's nerves were stretched to breaking point. And when Susan mentioned a photography special going on at the mall and suggested they take the baby there to have his picture taken, Robbie found herself frantic to have it done.

Didn't all new parents have portraits of their babies? Wouldn't it make them seem like more of a real family, more solidly parents, if they took their son in to have his portrait taken?

At the very least, this way she'd have some pictures of her baby if the judge took Joey away from them tomorrow morning.

Con didn't see things that way.

"Let's wait till he's ours," he said when Robbie cornered him in the kitchen and mentioned Susan's idea.

She held Joey a little tighter. "He *is* ours."

Con turned back to the glasses he'd been filling with ice. "It's just one more day, Rob."

"One more day might be too late."

As she finally voiced what had been in the back of both their minds all weekend, his only reaction was a stiffening of his shoulders.

"Get him ready," he finally said.

Robbie left the room without another word.

They were in line for the pictures when Robbie discovered that Joey's security blanket was missing.

"It's in his crib," Con said, holding his son up above his head. He'd been entertaining the baby with such antics ever since they'd arrived at the mall.

Robbie had visions of the baby starting to cry just when it was his turn in front of the camera. Without his blanket, she'd never be able to calm him. "We need it," she said.

"He hasn't missed it, honey. He'll be fine," Susan said, smiling as she watched Con with the baby.

But Robbie dug in her heels. "We don't know how much longer it's going to be, and if he gets tired, he'll want it," she said, certain Joey could miss it any second. "I'm going to go get it."

"Wait." Con handed the baby to Robbie. "I left it. I'll go," he said, pulling his keys from his pocket.

Joey in her arms, Robbie nodded. "Thanks."

"Robbie!" Stan stepped up to his daughter. He'd been watching the exchange silently till now. "You can't really expect Con to drive all the way back to the house just for some little scrap of cloth."

"She can when she's right," Con told Stan. "The blanket's the one constant in Joey's life. He should have it."

"You don't have to let her run you in circles, boy!" Stan said, frowning as he looked between his daughter and Con. "We're not going to be here *that* long."

Robbie wanted to curl up and die.

"My relationship with my wife is my business," Con told Stan, rendering the older man speechless. He'd never spoken to her father that way.

"I'll be back as soon as I can," he said to Robbie before striding off across the mall.

In that moment, standing there with her parents, holding Con's son, Robbie felt married for the very first time.

ONE DAY AT A TIME. It was how he'd always lived his life. Sometimes one hour at a time. Monday morning he was taking it one minute at a time. And he was thankful that Robbie was spending the minutes with him.

He had no idea what the future would bring. Whether they'd get custody of Joey, whether they'd ever have sex with each other again. He couldn't even think about where their marriage might take them, or for how long. Not today. It was one minute at a time. With all the minutes leading directly to the judge's chamber and the verdict he would reach.

"We need to go," Robbie said softly, standing as she put out the cigarette he'd lit a moment before. She was wearing the same denim skirt and pink blouse she'd had on the day they'd first met Joey.

She picked up their coffee cups. "We don't want to be late."

Con looked around him at Joey's things, the high chair he was still too young to use, the bottles on the counter, and nodded.

"We'll have to find a cupboard for those," Robbie said, following his gaze.

"Yeah." He hoped to God she was right.

He needed—oh, how he needed!—to pull Robbie into his arms. He needed to hold her, to feel her warmth, her confidence. He needed to comfort her, to assure her that he'd take care of everything, that he'd find a way to make her happy again.

Except that he couldn't. He couldn't touch her. Not

ever again. And he couldn't make her happy, either. He grabbed his suit coat off the chair and pulled it on.

"We have to take your car," Robbie said, following Con out to the garage.

"Right." But he knew that all the positive thinking in the world might not be enough today. Joey's car seat wouldn't be necessary if they were going to be coming home alone.

The drive to the courthouse was silent, as much of the morning had been, both of them drawing on the strength of the other, yet afraid to test that strength by voicing the fears, the doubts, the uncertainties that were forefront in their minds.

Con still hadn't told Robbie about Cecily; the moment had never seemed right. And there was no point telling her right now. Why add to her worries? If they didn't get Joey, she'd need never know, anyway. And if they did, the news of his biological mother's reentry into their lives wouldn't hurt so much if she heard it with Joey in her arms, already in her care. Besides, there was another six months of waiting ahead before they knew what kind of impact, if any, the woman would have on their lives.

They needed to worry about placement first.

One minute at a time.

ROBBIE'S STOMACH was cramped by the time they reached the courthouse. Her future had never been more insecure, and there wasn't a damn thing she could do but wait. Except...

"If we get him, we're staying married," she whispered to Con as they walked down the hall to the courtroom.

She'd had no idea how badly she'd needed to say those words until they were out.

"We'll talk about it later," Con said, looking straight ahead as they walked.

"We'll talk about it now, Randolph. I am not going in there to lose that baby or lose my place in both your lives when we come out."

He glanced down at her and then ahead again. They were almost there. "What place is that?" he asked, his frustration obvious.

"I don't know," she answered honestly, "but I'm not losing it." Before he could say another word, she sped up to enter the courtroom in front of him.

CON SAW a young blond woman turn to look at them as they walked in. She was sitting with a man he didn't know. He didn't recognize her, either, at first, only felt an instantaneous alarm, a sense that she was someone he never wanted to see again. She smiled at him.

And then he knew. Cecily Barnhardt.

He felt sick with dread. He didn't want to see her. Didn't want to have any connection with her. Ever. Didn't want Robbie to see her.

What was she doing there? He hadn't thought there

was any reason to expect her to be present. She'd already signed away her rights. And even if she was unsigning them, if such a thing was really possible, she still had six months to go of proving herself.

Didn't she?

With his mind in turmoil, Con followed Robbie to the front of the room and took a seat beside her. How could his wife sit beside him when a woman he'd had sex with, made a baby with, was four feet away, smiling at him as if she'd like to do it again?

"Who is she?" Robbie whispered.

His throat thick, Con stared at Robbie.

He didn't know what to say, couldn't get even a name past his lips. He didn't want her to know that this was the woman he'd taken to bed and forgotten. Shame filled him. And bone-deep regret that he was bringing Robbie further and further into his world.

He was saved from answering when the judge chose that moment to enter the room. The hearing had begun.

ROBBIE'S HEART pumped in double time as the judge took his seat. The woman across the aisle was momentarily forgotten as Robbie studied the elderly judge's face. Was that disapproval in his eyes as he glanced their way? Or merely speculation? Had the man already made up his mind?

Con was the first to be called to the stand. Robbie grabbed his hand and squeezed it as he stood up. She'd sworn to herself she wouldn't ever reach out to him again, but she couldn't send him to the wolves alone. He'd proved many times over the weekend, over the years, what a good man he was, what a caring man.

The judge asked Con questions about his job, about his home, looking at the pictures Con's attorney produced of Joey's nursery, of the clothes hanging in his closet, the toys they'd purchased, the high chair in the kitchen. Con sat stiffly in the witness stand, answering all the judge's questions in monosyllables. Robbie stared at the judge, her stomach in knots, still unable to guess what the man was thinking.

"And what support can you offer this child?" the judge asked, frowning as he looked through his half glasses at the papers in front of him.

"You have my financial statement," Con said.

Robbie groaned silently at the faint look of annoyance on the judge's face. She ached for Con, for how hard this was for him, for how inadequate he felt. He'd been tried and found wanting all his life.

But he was going to have to do better than this if he hoped to win his son.

"Yes, I see, Mr. Randolph. Well, thank you. You may step—"

"The boy needs more than money can buy," Con interrupted the judge. The older man turned, peering at Con over his glasses. Robbie held her breath.

"He needs to know he's wanted. That he belongs simply by nature of the blood running through his veins."

Yes. Tears burned the backs of Robbie's eyes as she listened to Con tell the judge about the thing *he'd* missed out on as a child. The only thing he'd ever really wanted. Something he never spoke about, never even acknowledged, but the most important thing he had to offer his son.

"He needs unconditional acceptance, the kind a kid can take for granted and not ever have to earn. The kind he'll never have if he starts out life abandoned by the people who gave him life. An acceptance only a biological parent can offer him." Con swung his gaze to the people in the silent courtroom. Robbie couldn't stop the tears from trickling down her cheeks as she watched him. Her strong silent husband had spoken from his heart.

He turned back to the judge. "This is the support I offer my son," he said, then rose from the stand and took his seat next to Robbie.

Unable to say a word, Robbie reached for his hand and held it, even when his fingers didn't curl around her own. He'd retreated deep into that place in his soul where he hid when he felt vulnerable.

The judge cleared his throat, took off his glasses and put them back on again. "May I have Karen Smith to the stand, please?" he finally said.

The next half hour was filled with the case workers' reports, nothing particularly damning, but nothing encouraging, either. Until Sandra Muldoon reported that Con had abandoned his son at birth.

"That's not true," Robbie hissed in Con's ear. She

hadn't had her chance on the stand yet, wasn't even sure she was going to get one at this rate, and she couldn't sit idly by and listen to these lies.

Con's muscles stiffened, his jaw so tight he couldn't possibly have said a word. He just shook his head at Robbie.

"That's her word against my client's, Your Honor." Con's attorney stood up. "My client had no knowledge of the child's existence until the state showed up on his doorstep last month."

"The child's mother told us she contacted the boy's father and was refused support," Mrs. Muldoon insisted.

"I understand the boy's mother is here?" the judge asked, looking over the courtroom.

Of course she isn't, Robbie thought.

Her gaze swung between the social worker and the judge. But even as she assured herself they were wrong, her heart froze, and she suddenly knew what was coming.

The woman who'd smiled at Con. That hadn't been the smile of a stranger.

"Yes, she's here, Your Honor." Robbie barely registered Mrs. Muldoon's words.

Ice filled her veins. If the judge had known the woman was going to be there, had Con known, too?

The judge called Ms. Cecily Barnhardt to the stand. Robbie couldn't look at the woman. She looked at her husband, instead. He didn't flinch, didn't show any reaction at all, other than resignation.

He'd known. He'd known and he hadn't told her.

There was no partnership between them. She was beginning to suspect there was nothing between them at all—except what her very fertile imagination produced. Had she simply conjured up what she wanted to see in order to justify forcing herself on him all these years?

And what chance in hell did they have of getting Joey if his biological mother was back in the picture? Or was she just there for testimony?

Why hadn't Con told her? Did she really matter so little? *And why should that come as any surprise?*

Con didn't look at Cecily Barnhardt as the judge started to question her, but Robbie couldn't look anywhere else. This was the woman Con had slept with, the woman who'd given birth to Joey.

"Tell us about your job, Ms. Barnhardt, your means of supporting the child."

Robbie tore her gaze away to glance at Con. Did that mean the mother *was* trying to get Joey back? Could she do such a thing?

Con, his face expressionless, continued to watch the judge.

"I'm not employed right now, but Joey'll be okay, anyway, with welfare and stuff," Cecily Barnhardt replied sweetly. "It's how I did it before."

She was everything Robbie had expected her to be. Con's type of woman exactly. Very beautiful and very feminine. And not very bright.

Robbie found it difficult to take much consolation

from this last, however. For Cecily was truly gorgeous. Her curves were luscious where they needed to be, accented by the spaghetti-strap sundress she was wearing. Her legs were long and tanned, tapering to slim ankles and dainty feet encased in high-heeled sandals. Even her toenails were polished.

And suddenly, Robbie wanted to be as far away from Con as the seat would allow. He'd hurt her for the last time.

If it hadn't been for Joey, she'd have walked out of that courtroom and just kept going. But she couldn't walk out on Joey. Even with her heart burning up with jealousy, she couldn't walk away.

Ms. Barnhardt's state-appointed lawyer showed pictures of the trailer where she lived. The judge declared it clean and rather sweet, but apparently it had no provisions for the baby.

"I just don't have the money for those yet," Cecily explained, and then looked straight at Con.

"Please, Mr. Randolph, I know you're a really nice man, buying me that hamburger and all and letting me sit with you so's I didn't have to be all alone in my trailer, even with you being so upset about that poor woman who died. You'll take care of me and my baby, won't you? Tell them you will, Mr. Randolph." Cecily's big eyes filled with tears. "Please?"

Con looked away.

"Tell us, Ms. Barnhardt," the judge said, clearing his throat, "exactly what did Mr. Randolph say when you told him about the baby?"

Cecily blinked. "Oh, I never told Mr. Randolph about Joey."

"But we have it on record that you said the baby's father refused support," the judge said, reading from the file in front of him.

"But that wasn't Mr. Randolph," Cecily said innocently. "That was Joe. We were s'posed to get married. Ever since I was fifteen. He was s'posed to be little Joey's daddy."

Con sat up straighter, watching the woman intently. Robbie watched, too, listening, taut with tension, and caring far more than she wished she did.

"But you named Mr. Randolph as the father on the birth certificate."

Cecily shrugged one slender shoulder. "Well, I had to. You can't tell lies in writing, you know."

Robbie felt more than heard Con sigh. His hand slid over her knee, searching for and finding hers. She didn't want his touch, didn't want it to mean anything, but that didn't stop her fingers from curling around his.

He continued to hold her hand while Betty Williams gave her testimony, stating that Joey had obviously had excellent care each time Robbie and Con had kept him. She mentioned the new clothes and toys Joey had come home with, said that Robbie and Con had left their phone number in case an emergency arose. She even told the judge how Joey had reached for Con the last time he'd gone to collect him.

And then it was Robbie's turn to take the stand.

She forgot Con. Forgot the mess they'd made of their lives as she fought for custody of the child who'd stolen her heart. Because whether Con wanted her or not was immaterial. In her heart of hearts, she truly believed that Joey would never have a better life than the one Con could give him.

Twenty minutes later, after listening to lawyers from all sides, the judge said he'd reached a decision. He asked them all to stand.

Con held tightly to Robbie's hand, telling her without the words he could never say how much the next moments meant to him. She squeezed his hand in return. Nothing mattered but the little boy whose entire future rested on the decision of one old man. Not her pain. Not Con's inability to love her.

"As Mr. Randolph so fluently pointed out, a child's biological parent can be an incredible asset to that child's emotional well-being. Which is why we hesitate to ever take a child from his mother's care if there's any hope that the child will find a loving home with her."

Robbie's heart sank as the judge paused. He looked at all three of them, his gaze serious.

"I feel that it is in Joey's best interests to give his mother, Cecily Barnhardt, six months to provide an acceptable home for her son."

No!

Con's grip crushed Robbie's fingers, but the tears that sprang to her eyes weren't from the physical pain.

"In the meantime," the judge continued, "I am

placing the boy in the care of his father and step-mother with final custody to be determined six months from today.''

Great sobs of relief racked Robbie's body as she threw herself into Con's waiting arms. He crushed her to him, lifting her right off the floor with the force of his embrace.

"Thank you," he said for her ears alone.

"You're welcome." And he was. Welcome in her life and in a secret part of her heart. Because in spite of the pain he'd caused her, the pain she feared he had yet to cause her, she was going to honor her wedding vows. She'd been standing by Con most of her life. She couldn't walk out on him now.

They had a son to raise.

CHAPTER THIRTEEN

BETTY WILLIAMS asked for a couple of hours for her family to say goodbye to Joey. The judge deferred her to Con.

He nodded his assent, partly because it felt so damn good to have the right to make the decision, but it still took everything he had to grant the request. He wanted his son at home. Now.

The future no longer seemed like a black hole. It suddenly had substance, a name. It had purpose.

And endless questions.

There were reams of papers to sign, details to go over. How soon could he have Joey added to his insurance? How often would they be bothered with visits from social services? Could they take him out of the state?

"He's really ours," Robbie whispered.

Warmth flooded Con, surprising him, almost scaring him for the brief second it took him to regain control. The same thing had happened to him in the courtroom moments ago, when the judge had told him he could have his son. But the feeling was just an aberration. A reaction to the changes that were taking place so rapidly in his life, which had been predictably the same for years. He wasn't falling back into that old trap again. He wouldn't start hoping. He couldn't. He was no longer capable.

Was he?

They still had an hour to kill after their business at the courthouse was finished. Con waited while Robbie went to a pay phone in the hall to give her parents a call and tell them the good news, and then walked with her out to his car.

She had something on her mind. He could tell by her sudden silence. He couldn't blame her if, now that it was over, she wanted out. Being a mother to Joey was hardly compensation enough for putting up with *him.* For withstanding a loveless marriage. He knew that.

Especially after he'd crossed that unforgivable line and used her body just for physical satisfaction. He'd known since he walked out of his bedroom the other night that it had only been a matter of time till she left him.

So why in hell did he still want to believe they could work something out?

"Where to?" he asked as they drove out of the parking lot. They didn't have time to make it home and all the way back to Gilbert in an hour.

"Someplace we can talk." Her softness was gone.

He glanced over at her, hoping to gauge where he stood, but she stared steadfastly out the windshield.

Without another word he pulled out into the traffic.

A pack of cigarettes lay open on the console between them. Open, but untouched.

Con knew the city as well as he knew the lines on his face, and twenty minutes later they were parked out in the desert on a secluded dirt track, not ten minutes from the Williamses' home.

If Robbie wanted out of their marriage, he had to let her go. Somehow. Hell, he should probably make her leave even if by some miracle she didn't want to.

He left the engine running, allowing the air conditioner to continue cooling the interior of the car. The scenery was barren, just brown flat land as far as the eye could see, with an occasional cactus or sagebrush. He wondered if this view of the desert Robbie had always loved was a portent of their future. Barren.

He reached for the pack of cigarettes, then threw it down again, thrumming his fingers against the steering wheel, instead. He wasn't going to smell like smoke when he picked up his son. But would he be picking him up with Robbie at his side?

He waited as long as he could, until his chest grew tight with the dread of what was coming. "So talk." His words finally cut the silence.

"Why didn't you tell me about her?" Robbie's voice was filled with accusation. And hurt.

Disconcerted, Con looked away. He'd actually forgotten about Cecily. About what Robbie must be thinking of him now that she'd come face-to-face with the side of him she'd always refused to see. He'd been too busy thinking about Joey. And about sex with Robbie.

So how did he explain why he'd kept silent when he didn't even understand why himself? Robbie had always been the only thing good and pure in his life. Cecily was the embodiment of everything else. Somehow he'd understood that it would all be over when the two met.

"You knew about her, didn't you?" she asked, her voice resigned, but bitter, too.

He nodded. And then added, "Not that she was going to be there today, though." As if that made any difference. He'd disappointed Robbie, hurt her. She was disgusted with the man he was. The type of man who would bed a total stranger and not remember it in the morning. Seeing Cecily had finally opened Robbie's eyes.

"But you knew she wanted Joey back?"

He nodded again, still thrumming, still not looking at her.

"Out of curiosity, were you ever going to tell me?"

"Of course!" he said, surprised into looking at her. Didn't she know he discussed everything with her? That he always had? Eventually. "If it became necessary."

"Necessary? Today it wasn't necessary for me to know that I was going to be seeing the woman you impregnated? That I wouldn't care? That it wouldn't faze me a bit?"

If she was trying to make him hate himself even more, she'd succeeded. "I'm sorry," he said. He didn't know what else to say. He'd been telling her all her life what a jerk he was.

His gut clenched when he saw the tears in her eyes. He could count on one hand the number of times he'd seen Robbie cry. And all of them because of him.

"You know, I believe you. You *are* sorry," she said softly, sadly. "But sorry isn't enough, Con. I had a right to know."

"Of course you did."

"So *why* didn't you tell me?" The anguish in her words confused him.

"Is that really what this is all about? Because I didn't *tell* you about her?" he asked.

"Yes!"

The relief he felt loosened his tongue. Maybe this time he could take away some of the pain he'd caused.

"I hoped she'd go away. That you'd never have to find out she'd appeared," he said, only just now realizing that that was what he'd been doing. Hoping. Even though he'd given up hoping years ago.

"You still should have told me, Con. I'm supposed to be your wife. Your partner in this thing. I should have been better prepared." Her tears continued to roll down her cheeks. There was so much pain. In her. In him.

Con pushed the console up and pulled her across the seat into his arms.

"I'm sorry, Rob." He wiped awkwardly at her tears with his thumb. "The time just never seemed right. The words wouldn't come."

She sat silently beside him, not pulling away, but not settling into his embrace, either. She needed more.

"I'm not proud of that night I spent with Cecily," Con said slowly. "Not eager for you to think less of me because of it," he finally admitted. To her. To himself.

She sank against him, turning to gaze up at him. "You sure you weren't just pushing me out of your life like you have everyone else you've ever known?"

"Hell, no!" He reeled back, shocked. "I can't imagine life without you in it, nagging me to death." He breathed a little easier when he saw a weak smile cross her lips. "And I don't push everyone else away, either," he felt compelled to add. "They leave of their own accord."

"Bullshit."

Feeling as though he'd just made it through a minefield, he wasn't up for a battle. "Was that it? The talk you wanted?" he asked.

"No."

She sat up, surprising him again. There was more?

"I didn't mean to bring her up at all," she admitted sheepishly. "She just slipped out."

He frowned. "What, then?"

"I want your word that we're in this for the long haul—you, me and Joey. I love him already, Con. I don't want to lose him."

He was right back in the middle of the damn minefield, after all. "As far as I'm concerned you'll always be his mother, no matter what happens between us," he said. Because it was only a matter of time before something did.

"I want your word, Randolph."

He turned away from her and looked out his side window. "I can't give it to you."

"Why?" The one word exploded into the car.

He looked back at her, his gaze impossible to misinterpret. "I think you know why," he said, looking her body up and down. He'd used her. Every inch of her. The memory of it drove him crazy in the dark hours of night. He hated himself for it. And for wanting to use her again.

"Because of the sex," she said bluntly. That was Robbie. Get the whole mess right out there on the table.

He nodded, still watching her.

"What about it?" she asked. He knew she was trying for nonchalance, but he heard the tiny catch in her throat.

"I still want it."

"Like it was last time?" Her gaze skittered away from him and then back.

"With me that's the only way there is." He couldn't lie to her. He'd never lied to her.

"It was horrible for me when you walked out of the room. You know that, don't you?"

His chest tightened as he saw the shadows in her

eyes, but she had to know. When words wouldn't come, he nodded.

"Are you going to force me?" she asked, sounding belligerent now.

"No." Forcing a woman to have sex was one of the few things he'd never done. Besides, with Robbie he wasn't sure he'd have to. He wasn't the only one who'd responded that night.

"Then we've got nothing to worry about, because I didn't much like your performance, Randolph. At least not there at the end." Her eyes welled up with more tears. "I've felt like many things in my time, but I've never felt like a whore before. It's not an experience I care to repeat."

Her words were like a slap in the face, one he knew he deserved.

"Trust me," she said, her voice filled with disgust. "It won't be happening again."

CON TOOK A LEAVE of absence from work for the rest of the month, and since Robbie hadn't taken time off for a honeymoon, she also stayed home that first week. Neither wanted to leave Joey with a sitter; neither wanted to leave Joey at all. They were natural parents, welcoming the change in their lives, adjusting to the sudden absence of freedom with very little effort. Joey was a godsend. He provided a dimension both of them had needed in their lives.

Con offered to make a grocery run Tuesday afternoon while Joey was napping. They were going through diapers more rapidly than either of them had anticipated, and running low on formula, too. But Robbie was well aware of his ulterior motive. He needed a cigarette. During the hour he was away, she was envious of the smoking he must be doing.

She heard him pull into the garage and met him at the kitchen door, ready to tease him.

"I left one lit in the car ashtray. I'll deal with the groceries," he said before she could get in a shot.

Robbie was out in the garage and in the front seat of his car in a flash. He hadn't left one lit. He'd lit a fresh one. She had an entire cigarette to savor.

How was she ever going to fall out of love with Con when he was so damn nice to her?

He had everything put away by the time she was back in the house, except for a package on the counter. She picked it up.

"What's this?" she asked.

He turned from the cupboard where they now stored Joey's bottles. "Nicotine patches. I figured they couldn't hurt," he said a trifle sheepishly.

She set the box down. "No. You're right. They'll probably make quitting a little easier on you."

His mouth quirked in that endearing half grin. "There's some there for you, too."

IT SEEMED there was plenty of everything for everybody as long as Robbie didn't ask for Con's love. As unconventional as their lives were, she was almost able to convince herself they were going to be just fine, the three of them. A happy little family.

Almost.

On Thursday afternoon she followed Joey, who the day before had discovered he could actually go places when he scooted on his belly, into Con's bedroom. It was just as Con came walking out of his adjoining bathroom, a towel around his neck.

He stopped, stark naked, and stared at her.

Heart beating an erratic tempo, she automatically sought the part of him she had no business looking at. She swallowed. The man was male perfection.

He didn't cover himself immediately. Not when he caught her gazing at him. Not even when his body started to react.

"Why didn't you shut your door?" she snapped. *Damn.* With one look she was on fire for him, weak with need, filled with desire.

He still stood there, staring right back at her. Then Joey scooted into his line of vision and he strode over to his dresser to pull a pair of briefs from a drawer.

He had the best ass she'd ever seen.

"What the hell are you doing in here?" he said.

Dry-mouthed, Robbie couldn't move, feeling more like an awkward schoolgirl than a mature woman. "Joey was exploring," she mumbled.

"I'll close my door in the future." Con's words were weary as he disappeared back into his bathroom.

Robbie grabbed the baby and ran.

Much of the week was fraught with tension. The

tension of unrequited love, of unfulfilled desire, of dying hopes and harsh realities. Robbie loved Con. He wanted her. But he was never going to love her back.

When Stan and Susan called, inviting them to Sedona on Saturday, Robbie jumped at the opportunity to get out of the house, to dispel some of the intimacy between her and Con. She was committed to her life with him, wanted it even. She was just going to need a little time to get over her love for him.

And he was going to need a night out now and then.

Nothing they couldn't handle.

The baby was asleep even before they hit the highway Saturday morning. He looked adorable in his baby-size blue-jean shorts and matching slugger shirt, his tiny face dimpled, even in sleep. He definitely had his daddy's chin. His new diaper bag, on the seat beside him, was stuffed with two more outfits and enough supplies to last them a week.

Con drove silently, his face a mask. Robbie wondered if he was happy—or at least *his* version of happy. Was he satisfied with the way things were working out?

"You getting anxious to get back to work?" she asked.

She hated not knowing what he was thinking, not knowing where she stood. Hated the lines she wasn't allowed to cross. Hated being dependent on him for any part of her emotional security.

He shrugged.

"There's not some case you're dying to crack? Some heathen to bring to justice?"

"There're always cases."

Her heart sank. Where was the man with a mission? The one who'd finally found a measure of peace with himself fifteen years before when he'd gone to work as a government agent?

The change in Con over the past couple of years really frightened her. She sometimes wondered if she was going to lose him completely to the purgatory that he'd forced himself to live in.

"Why don't you get out, Con?" she asked, unable to let it go. "No one said you had to be an agent forever."

"It's what I know."

She fiddled with the hem of her cutoffs. "But you hate it, don't you? Ever since that Ramirez deal last year."

"I'm good at it."

"You'd be good at anything you put your mind to."

He continued to drive, saying nothing, the cords in his neck tightening.

"It scares me to see what's happening to you," she said, daring to tread where she knew he didn't want her. But someone had to. "You used to take pride in your work. But now it's more like you hate yourself for doing it."

"I'm fine. Leave it." His voice had an edge of steel.

"Right."

They drove silently for miles. Robbie kept telling herself to let it go, to think about Joey, about their future. About being part of a family, instead of living alone.

"How are you going to love Joey if you can't love yourself?" she finally said into the stillness.

"I care for him just fine."

"Caring's not love, Con. Caring's lukewarm, detached. He needs total commitment."

"I'm committed."

She needed to holler at him, except that their baby was sleeping right behind them.

"We need your *love*, Con," she said, too upset to mind her words.

But he minded them. Plenty. "We?" he said, his voice hard, filled with ice. "You know my limits, Rob. You've always known them. I told you a long time ago that I'd never be that knight you were looking for."

What he'd told her was that he didn't believe in love. "You were just a kid then."

"I was never really a kid."

Anger swept through Robbie, anger at the life he'd had, the circumstances that had drained him of the things everyone needs—faith and hope and love. And anger at him, too.

"You want to be loved, Randolph. You've always wanted to be loved. Everybody does."

"Leave it, Rob," he said wearily.

"And what's more, you've got a little boy sitting back there who's going to idolize the ground you walk on," she continued, not even pausing for breath. "He's going to love you. And he's going to need your love in return. If you break his heart, you'll be no better than the people who broke yours."

He didn't say a word, just kept driving, jaw clenched so tight it was a wonder he didn't crack his teeth. She thought about what he'd said to the judge on Monday, about a kid deserving and needing to belong without having to earn the right. What he'd really been talking about was needing to be loved— unconditionally. He'd spent his entire childhood trying to earn that kind of love from anyone who might have some to spare. And he'd failed. Every time. Except with her. But that was the one place he'd never looked.

"It's time to quit running scared, Con," she said, her heart softening as she watched him. "It's time to allow the possibility that love is real. Because the only way you're going to get it or be able to give it is to believe it's there."

Con sent her a look that sparked real fear. Fear for him. For all of them. "You done?" he asked.

She wasn't reaching him. "Yeah."

So where did they go from there?

THE SKY CLOUDED OVER while Stan was cooking steaks on the grill. By the time they were eating dessert, winds were whipping across the land at well over seventy miles an hour, throwing debris across the yard and against the windows of the house.

"You can't drive home in this," Susan said, glancing worriedly out the dining-room window. She was holding Joey, sneaking him spoonfuls of her vanilla ice cream.

Robbie glanced at Con. There was no way they could stay. Her parents only had one spare bedroom. And Susan thought their marriage was normal.

But they'd be foolish to drive into the middle of a monsoon, to risk Joey's life. "If we had my truck—"

"We'll stay," he said, pushing his unfinished apple pie à la mode away. He didn't look any happier about the prospect than she did.

THOUGH STAN WAS strangely reluctant, Susan was delighted to have her family stay over. She fussed over them, producing a couple of toothbrushes, putting fresh sheets on the queen-size bed in the guest room, even though Robbie was certain the ones she replaced were clean. And she gave Robbie a nightgown—silk, with spaghetti straps and lace.

The baby was asleep in the middle of the queen-size bed and Con was in the bathroom, giving her time, Robbie knew, to get herself safely under the covers. Her nerves already on edge, the feel of the nightgown as she moved almost sent her out of her skin. The silk skimmed sensuously across her breasts, her stomach, her thighs, leaving a pool of warmth in its wake.

Why couldn't it have been a flannel nightgown?

She was considering changing back into her overalls, sleeping in her clothes, when she heard the bathroom door open down the hall. Diving for the bed, she snuggled close to Joey, pulling the covers up to her chin. Her problem didn't really lie with the nightgown. She could be wearing galoshes and a winter coat, and she'd still be nervous about sleeping with Con. It just wasn't smart.

Her eyes were squeezed shut when he entered the room. She was incredibly aware of him—the sounds he made, the tangy smell of his aftershave. She couldn't risk looking at him, too. Not here. Not now.

"He still asleep?" Con asked softly, closing the door behind him.

"Uh-huh." She kept her voice low, as though she was almost asleep herself.

"You want me to sleep on the floor?"

And admit that she was the least bit tempted by him? After she'd assured him that she no longer had any interest in his kind of sex? "Of course not. The bed's big enough for three," she said.

The light went out and the covers rustled as he pulled them back and climbed in on Joey's other side. He was lying in the same bed with her. For the very first time.

Robbie was almost afraid to breathe, to attract his attention, holding herself stiffly so she wouldn't risk running into him somewhere on the mattress. She had no idea what he was wearing—or if he *was* wearing anything.

"Good night," he said, the words clipped.

"Night."

Ten minutes later her muscles were cramped from her frozen position, and Con was sound asleep. For once Robbie envied him his control. He issued an edict to sleep, and he slept. She had a feeling she was still going to be awake when the sun rose.

But eventually, lulled by the even breathing of her new son, of her recalcitrant husband, finding comfort in their nearness, she slept.

CHAPTER FOURTEEN

HER LEG WAS WARM and silky smooth against his foot. He traveled the length of it with his toes, inching under the silk that covered her at midthigh and then making a return journey. Only to begin again. His hand found her curved hip beneath the covers and cupped it, moving a little lower to squeeze her thigh. The warmth between her legs tempted him, lured him to delve further. She was more woman than any woman he'd ever had.

Her body shifted, angled so that her hips were just inches away from his straining groin. He knew he should stop. He just couldn't remember why. At the moment nothing seemed more important than his body finding solace inside Robbie's.

When her fingers found his penis, caressing his length, he knew they'd come too far to stop.

He pulled away and sat up.

"Con?" Her whispered word was an invitation— and a plea.

"Let me move him," he whispered back, sliding his arms carefully beneath the baby sleeping soundly between them. They had another hour before Joey would wake up for breakfast.

Con had Joey ensconced in the middle of the love seat across the room, pillows packed firmly around him and on the floor beneath him, and was back in the bed in a flash.

"Are you sure this is what you want?" he asked, telling himself he was being noble even while his hands moved over her body, distracting her.

"Yes." Her soft acquiescence was filled with the same ache that was driving him. He needed her too much to care about right or wrong. To care whose house he was in or think about promises he'd made— and already broken. She was willing. He was going to take her.

He was only wearing briefs, and he quickly stripped them off, then did likewise with Robbie's nightgown. Her breasts seemed to beg for his touch and he was only too willing to comply. He sought the tiny scar that was all that was left of Robbie's run-in with Blackwell's dog, first with his finger and then with his lips, kissing it better before moving on. Her breasts were smooth and full, enticing him to taste. She was all woman. *His* woman.

And then, before he could reflect on that thought, on the fact that he'd even *had* that thought, he mounted her.

"I love you," she murmured, gazing up at him.

Con froze. This wasn't about love. It had nothing to do with love. It was sex. Plain and simple.

"I'm not asking you to love me back," she said.

"But I can't do this the way you want to, Con. I can't hold back the most important part."

He rolled off her and off the bed in one movement, her words like a bucket of ice water thrown on his body. "I'll see you at breakfast," he said, grabbing the shorts and shirt he'd worn the day before and heading for the shower. She couldn't love him. He couldn't let her.

Because while he could give her his body, he couldn't give her his heart. He didn't have one.

ROBBIE HAD NO IDEA how she made it through breakfast with her parents, thankful only that it couldn't be a leisurely meal as Stan and Susan were on their way to church. And since she and Con only had the clothes they'd worn up the day before, they couldn't accompany them. They were back on the road to Phoenix by eight o'clock.

Con hadn't driven five miles before he turned off onto a secluded dirt road. Joey, who'd fallen asleep almost as soon as they'd put him in his car seat, didn't budge when the car came to a stop beside a couple of evergreen trees.

Robbie's heart sped up, afraid of what was coming.

With one arm along the back of the seat, Con turned to look at her, his eyes serious.

"I can give you my protection," he said. "You're welcome to whatever money and possessions I've accumulated, whatever comes in the future. I can give you my body, and my loyalty..."

Robbie's heart was breaking as she sat there and listened to him. Because she knew what was coming. Knew what he would not be including in that list. Knew that no matter what he offered her, it was never going to be enough.

"I need love, Con," she said softly, the words sticking in her throat. "*Your* love." There was no hiding from it any longer, no more pretending he wasn't aware of how she felt about him. She just wasn't strong enough for both of them.

"You're welcome to everything I have, Rob."

"Yes, you said—all your possessions, your body and your loyalty. Thanks, but it's not enough, Con. I need your love, your heart."

He stared at her silently for a moment, his lips moving without sound. "It's gone," he finally said.

And for the first time Robbie believed him. Not because she didn't still think that Con was capable of loving someone, but because he truly believed he wasn't.

"It withered away, little by little, Rob," he continued. "Until I woke up one day and just didn't feel it there anymore. And you know what?"

She shook her head.

"It was a relief."

Robbie had never heard anything sadder in her life. She was bone-deep sad, too sad even for tears.

"I can't live like that," she whispered. "I thought maybe I could, but I can't." The blue sky and sunshine outside the car was filled with promises, with brightness and hope. She looked out, trying desperately to find a thread of that hope, to keep believing, but nothing happened. Her heart was as dark as the night had been.

He didn't say a word. He just sat there, watching her. Waiting.

"I'll stay with you until the custody hearing, until we're sure Joey's yours, but that's it." She'd make it through the next six months. Somehow.

And then she'd find a way to leave him, find a way to care for Joey like any other divorced parent. Because if she didn't, she was going to end up just like Con—a walking corpse.

"OK, LITTLE MAN, today we decide what we're going to do with the rest of Daddy's life." Con lifted his son off the changing table, talking to him as had become his habit in the past three days. Robbie had returned to work the day after they'd come back from Sedona, leaving Con alone with the baby.

"The month's up. I'm due back at the office tomorrow. And you, my boy, get to go to day care."

He wasn't overjoyed about Joey being in day care, but there was little choice. The baby gave him a happy toothless grin, cooing and gurgling. Con took the response to mean that the boy understood every word. He put Joey into the denim baby carrier he'd bought on Monday, his first day alone with the child, when it had seemed like he wasn't going to accomplish anything the entire day. Then, strapping the pack to his back, he got the vacuum cleaner out of the closet.

"The work I do in law enforcement is important. I'm good at it," he said, plugging in the cord, then turning on the switch. "It might give you something to be proud of someday—before you find out what a louse your old man really is." The hum of the cleaner drowned out his words.

The telephone rang a few minutes later and Con turned off the vacuum. The baby was pulling his hair.

"Randolph," he barked into the phone. Robbie wouldn't be calling. She was avoiding him as much as possible. And there wasn't anyone else he wanted to talk to.

"Hello, Mr. Randolph. This is Karen Smith."

Especially not her.

"Yeah?"

"I just wanted to let you know we've heard from Joey's mother again, sir, and she says she doesn't need to set up visits with Joey."

"She's relinquishing her rights?"

"She didn't say that, sir, only that something else has come up and she wouldn't need to be setting up any visits."

Con didn't like the sound of that. "Is this common?" he asked, grateful for the weight of the boy on his back. Joey was with him. He was safe.

"To be honest, no, it isn't. But Cecily's a little...different. All I can tell you is she sounded happy. And if there's no more contact from her, I suspect the judge will waive the six-month waiting period to give you and your wife permanent custody.''

"Good. Great," Con said, his mind racing. He'd move mountains to know that Joey's future was secure. And to be able to free Robbie to get on with her life, to learn whether he'd really destroyed her optimism as it seemed, or if, once she was away from him, she'd regain it. He'd give anything to make her happy again, and Karen's news was a big step in the right direction.

So why wasn't he overjoyed?

ROBBIE GOT the unenviable job of dropping Joey off at the day-care center the next morning. She and Con had chosen the place together, weeks before, and both were confident it was the best facility Scottsdale had to offer, but it was still a wrench to leave the baby with strangers again. She wished Con was with her. He'd have made the whole thing seem so commonplace with his unemotional logic. But he'd been called in to the office at six that morning. Apparently some information had come in during the night, and Con's men had needed his expert assessment before formulating a game plan.

His job was the one thing they'd been able to talk about with any normalcy the night before. Con had finally figured out that he didn't do his job just because he was good at it or because it was the one thing that had ever made him feel good about himself; he did it because he liked the work. Or most of it.

But it was time for him to get out of the field. To take one of the many promotions they'd offered him over the years and do what he did best—plan. Strategize. And leave the fieldwork to guys who'd seen a little less, who still had some illusions, who hadn't had the heart sucked out of them.

"I'll be back for you lickety-split, little buddy," she said, kissing the baby as she unbuckled his seat from her truck, making certain that his security blanket was tucked beside him. "Mommy just has one story to write up and then we'll do lunch. How does that sound?" she asked. Joey grinned at her and shoved his fist in his mouth.

Anna Lewis, the woman who'd registered Joey all those weeks ago, was waiting for them, and she whisked Joey away long before Robbie was ready to say goodbye. Filled with panic for a second, she almost ran after him. Joey had already spent too much of his life with strangers. Her only consolation was that she'd be back before lunch.

"It gets easier." Anna was back, a sympathetic smile on her face.

Robbie flushed. "I'm sorry, was I that obvious?"

Anna nodded. "But don't apologize. It's when the parents can't wait to get out of here that we worry."

"You'll make sure he has his blanket at all times?" Robbie asked, straining to see the room where Joey had been taken.

"Of course. Now, if you'll just sign him in?" Anna pushed a clipboard across the reception desk.

Robbie scrawled Joey's name, taking a little license and putting him down as Joey Randolph. He would be soon enough.

Sooner than they'd expected, according to what Con had told her about Cecily over dinner the night before. It hadn't seemed to faze him a bit that that meant she'd be leaving sooner. In fact, he'd seemed almost relieved. Not that she blamed him. The situation had been pretty unbearable between them since Sunday.

So why wasn't she relieved, too?

She pushed the clipboard across the desk. "I'll be back no later than eleven," she told Anna. And with one last longing look at the nursery door, she hurried out to her truck.

Joey was safe and that was all that mattered. She was going to have to get used to leaving him. It was soon going to be a way of life.

She cried all the way to the office.

CON WAS ENGROSSED in the contents of a file when the call came.

"Mr. Randolph? This is Anna Lewis at Rosemount Day Care."

Con stiffened, instantly alert. The woman sounded upset. "What's happened?"

"It's Joey, sir. He's gone!"

"What do you mean, gone?" he yelled.

"He's disappeared, Mr. Randolph." The woman gave a sob. "We can't find him anywhere!"

Con was out of his seat, reaching for his keys. "Have you called the police?"

"We thought maybe you'd want...since you're FBI and all..."

"I'm on my way," he said, slamming the phone down and running from his office.

He barked orders as he flew down the hall and out into the hot August sunshine, leaving a flurry of activity behind him. He wanted Cecily Barnhardt's ass found. Immediately. And an APB put out on his son. He wanted the airports and bus stations staked out. The highways blocked. He wanted Robbie.

The jacket of his suit caught on the door as he climbed into his car, and Con yanked it free, ripping the material. He shoved his key into the ignition and roared out of the parking lot and down the street, his heart racing, his thoughts tripping over themselves.

Would Cecily have done this? And if not her, who?

What was the possibility of a misunderstanding? Of the boy having simply been misplaced in the arms of one of the day-care workers, of him being there waiting for Con when he arrived? Slim to none.

He ran through his mind a list of all the people who had it in for him, but couldn't begin to calculate the possibilities. There were hundreds of people who'd threatened him over the years, who could have taken his son to get back at him. Hundreds of unsavory hate-filled people. Evil people who wouldn't think twice about...

It had to be Cecily. The woman was a little off, but

she was as gentle as they came. Please, God, let it be Cecily.

Wherever Joey was, whoever he was with, there better not be one mark on him.

Did he have his blanket?

Panic seared him as he swung into the day-care parking lot. Panic and despair so unbearable he almost collapsed beneath its weight.

Except that his son needed him.

He climbed out of his car and raced to the building.

THIS ISN'T HAPPENING. *It's all a mistake. It can't be happening.* The words rolled through Robbie's mind over and over, a litany that preserved her sanity until she met Con outside the front door of the day care. One glance at his face and she couldn't breathe. He looked haggard, ten years older than he had that morning.

So it *was* true. Joey was missing.

"No!" The word tore from her throat just as Con's arms wrapped around her.

Robbie pressed against him, aware only of the steady beat of his heart beneath her cheek.

"We'll find him," she said then, afraid to let go of Con, afraid she'd fall to a heap at his feet, unable to help him. To help Joey.

She felt Con's nod, but more, she felt the desperation in his grasp as he held her. "If they hurt him, I'll kill them." His voice was pure steel, and shaking with emotion.

Absurdly, the thought crossed Robbie's mind that a heartless man wouldn't shake with emotion.

"Let's go in," Con said, releasing her to open the door.

Anna was waiting for them inside. Her pretty face was blotchy, strained, streaked with tears. "I'm so sorry," she cried, wringing her hands. "This kind of thing doesn't happen here."

"Where was he last seen?" Con asked.

"In there," she pointed to the nursery door Robbie had watched her take Joey through earlier.

She followed as Con and Robbie hurried into the room.

"When?" Robbie asked.

"Nine-thirty or so. He'd just gone down for a nap."

It was ten-fifteen. He could be anywhere by now.

Three policeman were surrounding an empty crib on the far side of the room, questioning several day-care employees. Con joined them.

"Where are the other children?" Robbie asked, remaining in the doorway. She was loath to go near the crib. She couldn't bear to be close to it, to know that Joey had been there. To imagine someone reaching down, snatching him...

"Most of them have gone home," Anna said, pulling Robbie back from the darkness in her mind. "Those whose parents we couldn't reach are in the playroom with Maria and Joy." Anna's voice broke.

"I'm so sorry, Mrs. Randolph," she said, starting to cry again.

Choking back her own sobs, Robbie turned from Anna and went to join Con. It was either that or rip the young woman to shreds. *Why in hell didn't she watch Joey better?*

"No one saw anyone unusual hanging around?" Con was asking the workers as Robbie walked up, wiping tears from her eyes.

Shrinking under Con's gaze, every one of the day-care employees shook their heads.

"The center's growing. We get new people almost every day," Anna said, coming over to them.

"Where was everyone?" Robbie asked. *Why weren't you watching him?*

"It was snack time," an older woman explained. "All the children were sitting at tables in the snack room, except the sleeping babies."

"One of you doesn't stay in the nursery?" A policemen asked.

The woman nodded, swallowing with obvious difficulty. "I do. I'd just gone down the hall to get another box of diapers. I'd used the last one," she said.

"How many babies were in here?" Robbie asked her.

"Three."

One of the policemen wrote on a pad he'd been holding.

"And the other two were untouched?" Con asked.

The woman nodded, her eyes flooding with tears.

Robbie exchanged a glance with Con, saw the confirmation of her fears in his eyes. Three babies asleep in a room. Only one taken. This wasn't a random kidnapping.

"Have you checked the windows and doors?" Con asked the policemen gathered around the crib.

"Yes, sir." All three nodded.

"And?"

"Nothing."

Just then a fourth policeman entered the room, and Robbie's heart sank, nausea overwhelming her when she saw the rag in his hand. "I just found this on the other side of the fence surrounding the playground. It was caught. Looks like someone tried to pull it loose," he said, bringing the material over to the crib.

Con stared.

"You recognize it?" the officer asked Con, holding up the bedraggled scrap.

Con's lips were pinched, his eyes bleak as he nodded.

Robbie fell against him, holding on to his arm as the world spun around her. A wave of blackness threatened, and then receded.

It was Joey's blanket.

CHAPTER FIFTEEN

LEAVING THE POLICE officers at the day care to continue the investigation, dust for fingerprints and comb the area behind the playground, Con followed Robbie home. He kept his eyes trained on his surroundings, looking for anyone he didn't recognize—or someone he did. But the neighborhood was quiet, as it usually was on a hot weekday morning. Even the boy who worked in the neighborhood had stayed in out of the heat.

He checked his mailbox as he drove up, but it was empty. At this point he didn't know whether to be relieved or not. If the kidnapper got in touch with him, he'd at least have something to go on.

Robbie had already gone in when he entered the kitchen, throwing his car keys down on the kitchen counter with such force they bounced off and onto the floor. He felt so helpless. So damn helpless.

"There's nothing at the front door or on the answering machine," Robbie said, rushing back into the kitchen.

Con found a pack of cigarettes in the back of his junk drawer and lit two. Robbie took one with shaking fingers.

"What do you think?" she asked.

"Let me make a phone call and then we'll talk." He didn't know what to think. Except that if he didn't stay busy, he'd go out of his mind.

He dialed the number by heart.

"Pete Mitchell."

Con breathed a little easier when his occasional and usually reluctant partner answered. Pete was the best there was at negotiating hostage releases.

"I may need your help," Con said, taking a long drag on his cigarette.

"Where?" Pete asked without a moment's hesitation.

"This isn't official," Con said almost reluctantly. He wasn't confident that Pete would still be willing to help when he found out it was *Con* who needed him, not the government.

"What's up? Is Robbie okay? And little Joey?"

"The boy's missing, taken from his crib at the day care over an hour ago."

"You home?" Pete's voice was sharp.

"Yeah."

"Anything there?"

Con knew what Pete was asking. Had there been any word from the kidnappers? "No."

"I'm on my way."

Pete hung up before Con even had a chance to thank him. But he would never forget how quickly Pete was willing to come to his aid. Con couldn't remember a time he'd reached out to someone, asked for something and not been rejected. Which was why he usually didn't bother asking. He just gave orders.

"He's coming?" Robbie asked.

Con nodded, sat down and pulled her onto his lap. Her face was lined with strain, with the effort it took to hold herself together.

"You got any ideas?" he asked her. He didn't tell her he was scared to death.

"Cecily."

Con nodded. He'd reached the same conclusion. "Why?"

"A man would've drawn attention. Someone would have remembered seeing him."

"And a man would've been strong enough to rip Joey's blanket free," Con added.

Robbie's short sandy hair was sticking up where she'd run her fingers through it. As he smoothed it down, a wave of helplessness washed over him again, paralyzing him. Every contact he had would be working on the case by now, but it wasn't enough. He needed the best.

And he was it.

"If Joey's with her, he's probably OK." Robbie spoke softly, like a child needing reassurance.

"Yeah. She's stupid, but she's not evil," Con agreed.

"At least when she abandoned him before, she took him to a hospital," Robbie said.

Con stubbed out his cigarette. "The state borders

are all being patrolled. And chances are good she didn't think to change her appearance."

Robbie sat up, turning to look at him, fear in her eyes. "What about Mexico? She could take him to Mexico."

"We'll find him, Rob. We'll get him back," Con promised, hoping to God this was one promise he could keep.

Con tried for the millionth time to remember more about the night he'd spent at the Pink Lagoon Motel with Cecily Barnhardt. He had to figure out what was going on in her head to prepare for what might happen next.

"All she wants is to be taken care of," he said, repeating what Karen Smith had said. His own memories of the woman were so damn blurry! "She was afraid of something that night, I think. And happy as a clam as long as I let her sit there. Maybe that's why she ended up at the motel with me," he said, his head hurting with the effort it took to remember. "I can guarantee that I fully intended to be alone—falling-down drunk, but alone—when I rented that room earlier in the evening."

"Judging from the way she acted in court last week, I'd say you're definitely on the right track." Robbie's head was a welcome weight against his chest.

"Which probably means she won't go far. That if we just sit tight, she'll be contacting us."

Robbie stood up, crossing to the living-room window to stare out. "You think she'll be willing to trade Joey for monetary support?"

"Maybe. She wants to be supported—I know that for sure." Con joined Robbie at the window. The neighborhood looked like a picture in a travel brochure—beautifully landscaped yards, modern stucco homes with variegated tile roofs beneath gloriously blue skies. Not a hint that something could be so terribly wrong.

Robbie started to shake. "We have to give her whatever she asks for," she said, her voice filled with the tears she'd been trying so hard to hold back.

"Pete's going to disagree with that," Con said, bracing himself against the tide of emotion that threatened his own control. "We'd just be reinforcing the danger of it happening again."

She turned to look at him, her eyes pools of sorrow, of fear. "We have to pay her, Con."

Swallowing the lump in his throat, Con pulled her into his arms. "We will. We'll do whatever's necessary."

THE MINUTES TICKED BY slowly, each one a lifetime, a hell on earth. Yet somehow the minutes became hours, and still the baby had not been found and still no one had contacted them. The longer the baby was gone without anyone contacting them, the greater the danger, Con knew. Pete had arrived, and it was past one o'clock when Con got a call from Martin Emerson, one of his agents.

"Cecily left town almost two hours ago," Con said, hanging up the phone. Pete and Robbie were sitting on stools at the breakfast bar, untouched cups of coffee in front of them. Con still couldn't believe that Pete had come rushing over the moment he'd called.

"Someone recognized her at the bus station. She's going by the name Cecily Armstrong."

"Does she have Joey?" Robbie asked, jumping up. Her arm knocked over the coffee in front of her, but she ignored the liquid as it spread across the counter.

Con grabbed a towel and wiped it up. "Emerson hasn't found anyone who could confirm that for sure, only that she was carrying a bundle that could have been a baby."

He threw the wet towel into the empty washing machine, adding soap, then switched the appliance on. It took everything he had not to jump into his car and go after the woman.

"Where was she headed?" Pete asked, frowning. Robbie was rinsing her coffee cup, her movements jerky.

"Flagstaff."

"She's probably there already."

"Or got off somewhere else. Emerson has men on that now."

"You want to go after them, right?" Pete said. Robbie turned around just in time to see Con nod.

"No!" she said.

"You don't dare leave, Con," Pete said, calm but

deadly serious. "The woman's unstable. She's not going to like it if she can't reach you once she makes up her mind to ask for whatever it is she wants."

It wasn't in Con's nature to sit back and let someone else conduct an investigation that was more important to him than all that had come before. But he realized the wisdom in Pete's words. He had a feeling that Cecily wouldn't talk to anybody but him.

The other two were watching him, waiting. He couldn't stand the pressure of their expectant gazes. He had to find something to do.

Without another word, he went out to the garage, gathered up a drill, a screwdriver and the child-safety latches he and Robbie had picked up weeks before. The way Joey was scooting around, he had no time to lose. He couldn't have the baby pulling all their pots and pans out onto the floor or finding something to hurt himself with.

PETE FOLLOWED ROBBIE into the living room. She'd heard Con wrestling with his tools out in the garage. And as soon as she'd known he wasn't going for his car, she'd decided to give him a little time to himself. Being alone was the only way Con knew how to deal with pain.

"Con's changed," the older man said.

"How do you mean, changed?" she asked, heading straight for the window, as though if she looked out long enough, the kidnapper would decide to bring Joey home.

God, please don't let him be hurt.

"I've wondered a time or two if the man ever felt anything at all," Pete said.

"Always," Robbie answered instantly. "More than anyone realizes."

Pete shook his head. "You could've fooled me. Don't get me wrong," he added when Robbie turned. "I've always respected him, admired his genuine self-lessness. I've just worried a time or two that he'd lost an important component in dealing with people. The *emotional* component."

Robbie nodded. She could understand that. She'd wondered a time or two herself. "I guess when all you see is ugliness, it's all you believe is there."

"Maybe." Pete shrugged. "But you and the baby have obviously convinced him differently. I've never seen him so broken up."

"I know." Robbie turned back to the window as a fresh bout of tears flooded her eyes. She just didn't know if the pain Con was feeling now would finally convince him he still had a heart or be the final nail in its coffin.

"He ran the washing machine for one little towel," Pete said, crossing to Robbie and putting an arm around her shoulders.

Robbie grinned through her tears, as she was sure Pete intended, and nodded.

They stood silently for a moment, until Con's curses started coming from the kitchen.

"Do you think it would be a good idea if I get

something put on the news? Just in case someone recognizes Cecily or Joey?'' she asked Pete suddenly. She had to do *something*.

''Can't see how it'd hurt,'' Pete said, considering. ''She's got to know we're after her. And maybe someone will see them.''

Pete stayed until after the film crew she called had come and gone. He even convinced Con to go on the air, to issue a plea to the kidnapper to return his son.

But the hours passed and still no word.

A CAR DROVE down the street. A black sedan Con recognized. His shoulders stiffened as his gaze followed the vehicle intently. It belonged to his neighbor across the street and disappeared into the man's garage. The knot in Con's stomach tightened. He couldn't stand much more of the waiting.

Jamming his hands into his pants pockets, he resumed pacing between the phone and the living-room window. Robbie was in the kitchen, where she'd been ever since Pete and the film crew had left, making a dinner neither one of them was going to eat.

His phone was wired, there were guards posted at each end of his street, and still nothing was happening. Had Joey been fed? Was someone changing his diaper?

Cursing, Con paused at the window yet again. The neighborhood was so quiet he couldn't stand it. Why did that damn kid who was always around have to

take today off? At least he'd be someone to look at.
At least there'd be something going on.

Images of what might be happening to his son in-
vaded his mind. The world was filled with sickos,
with evil people who wouldn't hesitate to hurt a tiny
child to get back at the child's father. People who—

Suddenly Robbie was there, her arms creeping
around his waist, holding him. She didn't say a word.
There wasn't anything *to* say. But she was there, sharing her strength with him, chasing away the grotesque
images that were haunting him more and more as the
hours passed.

Cecily should have contacted them by now.

Con turned, sliding his arms around his friend. His
wife. He needed her now in a way he never had before, needed her heart, her soul. Her gentle caring.
Her eternal optimism.

He needed her if he was ever to find a way to hope
again.

ROBBIE HELD CON, taking as much comfort from him
as she gave. He was a rock, solid, sure. Capable of
moving mountains. He always got his man. Always.

She wasn't sure exactly when his need changed,
when she sensed a more immediate urgency, a physical urgency, within him. Without consciously knowing she was doing so, she floated from feeling a sense
of comfort to feeling a desperate mind-numbing desire.

Desperate for the escape, she clutched him to her

as he lowered his lips to hers. *Let him take me away, let him make me forget. Just for a minute. Let me forget.*

She kissed him hard, searching for something beyond the sex, some affirmation of a greater power, for the bond of strength born when two people become as one.

Stopping only long enough to close the living-room curtains, Con stripped her silently and lowered her to the floor. There was no foreplay. No patience for leisurely exploration, no time. Only the compulsion to connect to each other, to take everything, to give everything, to share the pain and fear that were eating them both alive.

Robbie didn't utter a word, either. She couldn't. There were no words for what they were seeking.

But they were seeking it together. Of that she was sure.

Con was powerful when he entered her, and she offered him sanctuary from the storm thrashing through him, finding her own sanctuary in the giving.

They could get through this. Together. They could do anything as long as they were together.

She flew with him to a place where only goodness and beauty existed. And she held on to him during the return to earth, to face again the pain of their missing son. But even in the midst of harsh reality, a miracle occurred. For Con didn't pull away from her. He didn't close his eyes or his heart. He stared straight into her eyes—and allowed her the first glimpse she'd ever seen of the man who'd been living alone inside him for more than thirty years.

"Thank you," he said, his eyes bright with the effort it was taking him to keep unfamiliar emotions from spilling over.

"I love you," Robbie whispered, suddenly knowing he was ready now to hear the words.

He nodded and crushed her to him. He might not ever be able to love her back, but at least he'd finally learned how to accept her love. To believe that someone could love him.

CHAPTER SIXTEEN

IT WAS MIDNIGHT and still no word. Con sat at his desk waiting for the phone to ring. Robbie was half reclining on the couch smoking a cigarette. She hadn't said a word in almost an hour.

He'd finally convinced her to call Stan and Susan before they had a chance to hear about the kidnapping on the news. They were on their way to Phoenix now. Con couldn't believe how anxiously he was awaiting their arrival. Not that their being here was going to make any difference to the kidnappers or to Joey's being found.

But they'd always been there for Robbie. They'd always kissed her hurts and made them better. Maybe Susan could at least talk her daughter into getting some sleep.

His heart slammed at the shrill ring of the telephone. Robbie jumped off the couch, rushing over to him as he picked up the receiver.

"Randolph."

He listened to the voice on the other end of the line with a sinking heart, avoiding Robbie's eyes as he hung up the phone. *Damn.*

"What? Who was it?" Robbie asked.

"Emerson. They found Cecily." He couldn't stand the hope he saw in Robbie's eyes. Couldn't stand the pain he knew was going to follow. It was time to get to work.

"She didn't have him," he said bluntly.

"Didn't have him?" Robbie echoed in disbelief, leaning against the desk.

"She'd run off with some guy who's old enough to be her grandfather. He's rich as hell and promising to take care of her for the rest of her life."

"Why the false name? The secrecy?" Robbie asked, obviously not willing to give up hope yet.

"They're running from his grandchildren, who're trying to have him declared incompetent. Apparently they want his money, too." Con wasn't surprised, just damn tired of the rotten things people did, the lengths they were willing to go to when greed was in the driver's seat.

And sick at the thought of the implications the phone call had put on Joey's disappearance.

"What about the bundle she was carrying? Maybe she dumped Joey someplace."

Con shook his head. "She didn't have a suitcase. She'd rolled up the things she was taking with her in the blanket from her bed."

"Oh, God..." Robbie's words trailed off and a look of despair crossed her face.

Con wanted nothing more than to pull her into his arms, to wipe that look off her face. But they didn't have another minute to lose.

"We have to get to work, Rob. I need your help."

BY THE TIME an exhausted Susan called them to breakfast in the morning, Stan, Robbie and Con had memorized every name left on the list Con had made of possible suspects. The list had been several pages long when Stan and Susan had arrived in the early hours of the morning. It was now down to one sheet.

"I'll get the newspaper," Susan said as soon as she'd filled coffee cups for all of them. "Robbie, Con, eat."

Neither of them had eaten since breakfast the day before.

Robbie didn't think she could choke down a bite of the food Susan had prepared. The sight of the eggs made her nauseous. The fluffy biscuits only made her think of Joey and the time she'd given him half a biscuit to gum. Most of it had landed on the floor, but the baby had had the time of his life.

"Con! Stan! Come here!" Susan called from just inside the front door.

Wiping tears from her eyes, Robbie ran into the foyer after them.

"There's an envelope here," Susan said, holding up the newspaper. A sheriff's wife for many years, she knew better than to touch the envelope that was nestled in the centerfold of the paper.

Grabbing a handkerchief from his pocket, Stan took the envelope. It wasn't sealed. All four of them stared at the single piece of paper that fell out and floated to the floor.

Taking the handkerchief, Con picked it up. As his eyes skimmed the page, the color drained from his face.

Stan read the note over Con's shoulder and headed for the bathroom. Susan grabbed a hold of Robbie before she collapsed.

"Let me see it," Robbie said.

With an arm around both of them, Con held up the letter.

I have the kid. All I can say is he's alive—for now. And he cries good. Real good. If you're patient I might even let you hear him scream a time or two. Or maybe not. Have a good day.

Whoever had the baby had taken him out of malice. He wanted to make them suffer.

"I've got some calls to make," Con said, his voice dead.

Robbie started after him, but Susan pulled her back. "Let him go, honey."

"He's blaming himself," Robbie said. "I can't leave him alone like this. It isn't his fault the world is full of sick people. He can't blame himself for…" Her voice broke as more tears came.

"He has to work through it on his own, Robyn," Susan said in a tone of voice Robbie had never heard her use before. "You can talk to him until you're hoarse and he still won't believe. He has to learn to like himself on his own.''

Feeling like a little girl again, Robbie buried her face against her mother's ample bosom, crying for all the wrongs there had been in one very good man's life. Crying, too, for the baby who was lying helplessly somewhere, crying, needing them.

By noon Con still had no idea who had taken his son. Throughout the morning most of the suspects on his list had been eliminated. A couple were even dead. And suddenly, despite his fear and exhaustion, the answer came to him. He remembered another threat he'd received. One he'd given no credence to whatsoever. A name that wasn't on his list.

''It's got to be the boy!'' he exclaimed. Every pair of eyes around the table swung to him. Pete was there, Stan and Robbie, as well as Martin Emerson, who'd returned from Flagstaff midmorning.

''What boy?'' Martin asked.

Just like that, things fell into place, the pieces of the puzzle fitting so perfectly Con knew he'd hit the mark.

''The woman who died last year in the Ramirez deal. She had a teenage son. He came after me at the funeral, refusing to let me in the church. Said he'd make me pay.''

''A boy, Con?'' Pete said doubtfully.

''He looked different then, had short hair, glasses.''

Stan leaned forward. ''You've seen him since?'' he asked sharply.

"He's been working in the neighborhood. Doing odd jobs. Started a few months ago."

Robbie's mouth fell open in shock. "The boy who does the Waverlys' yard?"

Con nodded, his adrenaline pumping. "I just realized it's the same kid. It wouldn't have been all that difficult for him to get into the day care. Could've said he was an older sibling if someone stopped him." Con's instincts were telling him to move. He'd found his answer. He had to save his son.

"He wasn't around at all yesterday..." Robbie's voice trailed off.

Emerson grabbed the mobile phone from the middle of the table and ten seconds later was barking orders into the receiver. Every available man in the state would soon be searching for the boy.

"Pete, I need to know everything you can tell me about dealing with a hostage situation," Con said. He was going to do this one alone. No one else was going to die as a result of his orders.

"Stan, find out if he's purchased a gun in the past fifteen months, or ammunition to go with a gun his mother may have had."

"Robbie, how many of your snoops can you get to work on finding him?"

Robbie was on her feet. "All of them," she said on her way out the door. "Give me an hour."

She was exhausted, her face haggard, and still she was full of optimism. Of hope. And Con suddenly found himself buying into that hope.

If his hunch was right, the kid's main purpose was to make Con suffer a long slow living hell. Which meant Joey was still alive. And that was all Con cared about.

"I'VE FOUND HIM!" Robbie rushed into the living room two hours later. "He rented a migrant shack at the back of an orange grove twenty miles east of here."

Con was on his feet instantly, grabbing Robbie by the shoulders. "You're sure?" he asked.

She nodded. "Positive. The guy who rented him the shack was the same one who tipped me about that story I did about the dead greyhounds last year. Apparently the kid's been fixing up the place for weeks."

Which only reinforced Con's theory. The boy planned to string Con on for a while, to squeeze every bit of suffering out of him. He wasn't going to settle for one nasty note. Which meant that in all likelihood Joey was still alive.

"I'm going after him," Con said.

"Wait a minute," Stan said, coming in on the tail end of the conversation. He and Pete had been in the kitchen coordinating a statewide search of gun shops by phone.

"He's armed. Bought himself a nice little automatic almost a year ago."

Robbie's eyes filled with fear as she looked from

her father to Con. "Let Pete go in first, Con. He's trained to deal with this."

"No," Con said. Pete had a wife, a son and another child on the way. He might even have become his friend over the past twenty-four hours. Con wasn't going to let him risk his life. "This is between me and the kid. I'm going alone."

In spite of all the warnings to the contrary, in spite of a direct order from his boss, Con left the house alone ten minutes later. He wasn't waiting for a full-scale move. He wasn't waiting for assistance to be organized. What he was doing, Robbie knew in her heart, was giving up his life. He was going to offer himself to the kid in exchange for Joey.

An eye for an eye. A parent for a parent.

She'd heard him on the phone in his bedroom right before he left. He'd called his attorney and named Robbie as Joey's legal guardian in case anything happened to him.

He hadn't even kissed her goodbye. And she understood that, too. They'd become one spirit, one soul, the day before. If he got too close to her, he might not have the strength to separate from her again. To do what he had to do.

What she couldn't let him do.

"Pete, we have to go after Con. We can't let him do this alone," Robbie said, bursting into the kitchen after watching Con's car drive away.

Pete put down the phone and picked up his keys.

"I've already called Emerson. They're going to meet us at the shack with backup," he said. "Let's go."

"Be careful," Susan said, hugging Robbie tight before pushing her out the door.

"Bring them both back alive," Stan said, and then picked up the phone. He was calling several of his former deputies to serve as additional backup. If the odds made any difference, they had a chance to pull this off.

But in law enforcement, the odds very rarely made a difference.

CON APPROACHED the shack on foot, his footsteps silent, like a panther on the hunt. The old one-room building wasn't air-conditioned, and the one window was wide open. Con heard the drone of a television, the steady hum of a high-voltage fan. Sweating in the hundred-plus temperature, he hoped to God the baby had survived the heat.

He was still wearing yesterday's slacks and shirt, with his holster strapped to his chest, and wondered if maybe he should have taken the time to change. The suit might intimidate the kid. It might make him do something crazy.

He could hear the television show quite distinctly by the time he reached the window. It was an old "Happy Days" rerun. Two fans were humming. There was no sound of Joey.

Slowly, so slowly he barely felt himself move, Con peeked inside. He saw the kid immediately. He was sitting in the middle of a newish-looking couch, frowning at the television set. A baby bottle, half-full of what appeared to be juice, was standing on an old barrel being used as a coffee table. A box of diapers, a size too big, stood open on the floor beside the couch. There was no sign of Joey.

The kid glanced back to a corner by the refrigerator, the open refrigerator, Con noted. The kid glanced that way again several more times over the next minutes. A fan had been set up to one side.

Homemade air-conditioning. The baby was somewhere behind the refrigerator door. Con was sure of it.

As it turned out, it was almost too easy to take the kid. Con used a trick so old it never worked on experienced criminals. He threw a rock just outside the door of the shack, and as predicted, the kid came out to investigate. Con had him in a half nelson before the kid knew what had hit him. Before he could aim the gun he had cocked in his right hand.

The gun went off, a bullet ricocheting against the dirt to lodge in the outside wall of the shack.

"Easy, now, easy," Con said.

The boy was much stronger and better-trained than Con had anticipated, but he managed to wrestle him to the ground, disarming him at the same time.

"You!" the kid cried when he got his first look at his assailant.

"I came for my son," Con said, holding both the kid's arms with one hand while he took off his belt.

"I should've taken the woman," the kid grunted, using a decent karate maneuver that just missed Con's groin. "I'd at least have raped her by now."

Con twisted the kid's arms further, securing them with his belt. "You hurt either one of them, you're dead."

He meant it.

A FLASH OF MOVEMENT warned Con they were no longer alone. Dropping the end of the belt, he ripped open his shirt and grabbed his gun. His finger was on the trigger, ready to fire.

"Hold it, buddy," Pete said, coming out into the open as he assessed the situation. Robbie was right behind him, followed by a dozen agents and officers.

Just then Joey started to cry lustily from inside the cabin. Con handed his secured charge over to Pete and ran in. He grabbed his son up into his arms, holding him tightly against his chest. And suddenly he started to shake.

Joey was safe. His son was really safe. *Thank God.*

Weak with relief, he cuddled the boy, crooning softly to him.

"It's OK, son, Daddy's here," he said, his voice breaking as the baby's wails slowed to whimpers and then stopped altogether. Joey studied Con, a frown between his tiny brows.

"Daddy's got you now, Joey. Daddy's got you," he said, aware only of an intense need for Joey to know that he'd always be there for him.

The baby lifted his hand and began bopping Con's cheek. Con reached up to take hold of the tiny fist and was startled to find his own face wet with tears.

In that moment he realized what he'd been feeling since the day Sandra Muldoon had knocked on his door.

"I love you, son," he said awkwardly, the words foreign to his tongue.

He was in love. With his own small son.

And with his wife.

He turned toward the door, looking for Robbie. He was going to do everything in his power, move the damn mountains she kept talking about if that was what it took, to make up to her for all the times he'd hurt her.

She was standing in the doorway, her face, too, streaked with tears. And she was, without a doubt, the most beautiful woman he'd ever seen.

"You said you love him," she murmured.

"Yes." Con felt vulnerable as he stood there, the baby his only protection.

"I'm glad." She smiled a radiant honest smile, asking for nothing at all. She was happy for him. Only him. And maybe a bit for the baby she adored, too.

The final dam in Con burst. He reached out a hand to her, daring to hope. She looked at his outstretched hand, and the seconds ticked slowly by while she glanced from his hand to his face, searching for something he hoped with all his being she'd find.

And then her fingers stole into his. He squeezed

them, looking into her eyes, allowing her to see into his. And into his soul.

She wrapped her arms around him, buried her face between him and the baby and began to sob. Con held her and let her cry, knowing she was shedding tears for both of them, ridding them both of years of stored-up pain.

Joey grabbed a fistful of Robbie's hair and gave it a yank worthy of the offspring of Connor Randolph.

"Ow!" she cried, lifting her head to grin at her son through her tears. "I can see we'll have to teach you how to treat a lady, young man," she told him, freeing her hair from the baby's grip, and keeping his tiny hand captive within her own.

"I'll never be a knight in shining armor," Con said, needing to get things settled once and for all.

"I never said I wanted one. *You* said I did."

"You deserve one."

"But all I've ever wanted was you." The baby squirmed. "Let's take our son and go home, eh, Randolph?" Robbie took the baby from him.

That was it. Just like that, with nothing more from him, she was going to come home with him, make them the family he'd always wanted. She hugged Joey to her breast, pressing quick kisses to his neck. Laughing when Joey laughed.

Con couldn't let her do it. Couldn't let her settle for less than she deserved, less than she needed.

"Rob?" She was halfway to the door, but turned back when she heard him call her name.

"Yeah?"

"I love you."

"I know you do." Her voice broke, her chin trembling, as he finally admitted what had been there between them for a lifetime.

"I love you, too," she whispered. "I always have."

Tears poured down her cheeks again as Con scooped the woman of his dreams up into his arms, baby and all, holding her beneath his heart.

The heart she'd given back to him.

EPILOGUE

ROBBIE SAT with her father on the closed-in porch in Sedona, watching for Con to come back with their son. He'd taken Joey up the mountain to find a Christmas tree.

"The boy's only two. You think he knows what he's looking for?" Stan asked, puffing on his pipe.

"I don't think he cares as long as he's with his daddy."

"I always knew that husband of yours would make a fine family man if he ever lost that chip he carried on his shoulder."

"I'm not doing too badly in the wife department, either," Robbie said. She was still bothered sometimes by the conversation she'd had with her father on this very porch eighteen months before.

Stan cleared his throat and looked anywhere but at his daughter. "I was wrong, girl. I was looking at what I'd raised you to be, and seeing you all alone and lonely, I got to thinking I done you wrong. That it was my fault you were suffering so from loving a man who wasn't loving you back."

Robbie smiled, rubbing her hands over her extended belly. "He loves me," she said.

Stan glanced up the mountain, embarrassed. "'Course he does."

"Did I tell you the kid who took Joey is in counseling?" Robbie asked, deciding to let her father off the hook—for now.

Stan harrumphed. He'd made his opinion clear as far as that kid was concerned. Stan thought he should have been tried as an adult, locked away forever.

"He still has another year in detention until he's eighteen, but he wants to go to college, start over and put the past behind him."

Stan harrumphed again.

The baby kicked Robbie in the ribs and she gasped slightly. She tried to push the huge mound into a more comfortable position. Except that at thirty-five weeks, there wasn't one. She was loving every minute of this pregnancy. And with all the miracles that had taken place in her life, she could afford to be generous.

"The kid went a little crazy when he lost his mom, Pop, but he's basically a good kid. He went out of his way to make sure Joey was all right the whole time he had him."

"He was going to kill him," Stan said, his words sharp.

Robbie shook her head. "I don't think so. I don't think he'd have hurt Joey. Or me, either. He just wanted Con to suffer. And he knows now that Con was already suffering over the death of the kid's mother. Con wrote to him once, told the kid what really happened that day, how it happened."

He was also planning to pay for the kid's college education, but Robbie didn't think her father was ready to hear that yet.

"He's a better man than I—"

Stan broke off when Robbie gave a little cry. Con's younger son was a mighty determined little fellow. He'd never kicked her so hard.

"Susan!" Stan bellowed, his face white as he watched Robbie.

"What?" Susan came running from the kitchen, drying her hands on a dish towel.

"She's—"

"It's nothing, Mom," Robbie interrupted. It couldn't be. Not until Con got back. She was not going through this without him.

"Connor, Jr., just kicked a little harder than usual." Robbie rose from her chair, hoping to make more room for her unborn son, just as Con came walking across the desert field in front her. Joey was riding on his shoulders, an evergreen dragging behind them. Robbie couldn't tell whose grin was broader, Joey's or Con's.

Another fierce pain gripped Robbie, followed by a flood of warmth between her legs.

"Oh!" Susan said, grabbing Joey from Con's shoulders when they came through the door. Stan, meanwhile, tried to steer Robbie to the couch.

She stood her ground, her discomfort unimportant, as her gaze sought and found her husband's.

"What?" he asked, crossing to her immediately.

The look in his eyes told her everything she needed to hear. She returned the look and said simply, "It's time."

EVER HAD ONE OF THOSE DAYS?

TO DO:

- [x] at the supermarket buying two dozen muffins that your son just remembered to tell you he needed for the school treat, you realize you left your wallet at home

- [x] at work just as you're going into the big meeting, you discover your son took your presentation to school, and you have his hand-drawn superhero comic book

- [x] your mother-in-law calls to say she's coming for a month-long visit

- [x] finally at the end of a long and exasperating day, you escape from it all with an entertaining, humorous and always romantic Love & Laughter book!

ENJOY
LOVE & LAUGHTER™
EVERY DAY!

For a preview, turn the page....

Here's a sneak peek at
Carrie Alexander's THE AMOROUS HEIRESS
Available September 1997...

"YOU'RE A VERY popular lady," Jed Kelley observed as Augustina closed the door on her suitors.

She waved a hand. "Just two of a dozen." Technically true since her grandmother had put her on the open market. "You're not afraid of a little competition, are you?"

"Competition?" He looked puzzled. "I thought the position was mine."

Augustina shook her head, smiling coyly. "You didn't think Grandmother was the final arbiter of the decision, did you? I say a trial period is in order." No matter that Jed Kelley had miraculously passed Grandmother's muster, Augustina felt the need for a little propriety. But, on the other hand, she could be married before the summer was out and be free as a bird, with the added bonus of a husband it wouldn't be all that difficult to learn to love.

She got up the courage to reach for his hand, and then just like that, she—Miss Gussy Gutless Fairchild—was holding Jed Kelley's hand. He looked down at their linked hands. "Of course, you don't really know what sort of work I can do, do you?"

A funny way to put it, she thought absently, cradling his callused hand between both of her own. "We can get to know each other, and then, if that works out..." she murmured. *Wow.* If she'd known what this arranged marriage thing was all about, she'd have been a supporter of Grandmother's campaign from the start!

"Are you a palm reader?" Jed asked gruffly. His voice was as raspy as sandpaper and it was rubbing her all the right ways, but the question flustered her. She dropped his hand.

"I'm sorry."

"No problem," he said, "as long as I'm hired."

"Hired!" she scoffed. "What a way of putting it!"

Jed folded his arms across his chest. "So we're back to the trial period."

"Yes." Augustina frowned and her gaze dropped to his work boots. Okay, so he wasn't as well off as the majority of her suitors, but really, did he think she was going to *pay* him to marry her?

"Fine, then." He flipped her a wave and, speechless, she watched him leave. She was trembling all over like a malaria victim in a snowstorm, shot with hot charges and cold shivers until her brain was numb. This couldn't be true. Fantasy men didn't happen to nice girls like her.

"Augustina?"

Her grandmother's voice intruded on Gussy's privacy. "Ahh. There you are. I see you met the new gardener?"

HARLEQUIN WOMEN KNOW ROMANCE WHEN THEY SEE IT.

And they'll see it on **ROMANCE CLASSICS**, the new 24-hour TV channel devoted to romantic movies and original programs like the special **Romantically Speaking-Harlequin® Goes Prime Time**.

Romantically Speaking-Harlequin® Goes Prime Time introduces you to many of your favorite romance authors in a program developed exclusively for Harlequin® readers.

Watch for **Romantically Speaking-Harlequin® Goes Prime Time** beginning in the summer of 1997.

If you're not receiving ROMANCE CLASSICS,
call your local cable operator or satellite provider
and ask for it today!

Escape to the network of your dreams.

ROMANCE CLASSICS

Reach new heights of passion and
adventure this August in

ROCKY MOUNTAIN MEN

Don't miss this exciting new collection featuring
three stories of Rocky Mountain men and the
women who dared to tame them.

CODE OF SILENCE
by Linda Randall Wisdom

SILVER LADY
by Lynn Erickson

TOUCH THE SKY
by Debbi Bedford

Available this August wherever
Harlequin and Silhouette books are sold.

Let's Celebrate!

LOVE & LAUGHTER™

invites you to
the party of the season!

Grab your popcorn and be prepared to laugh as we celebrate with **LOVE & LAUGHTER**.

Harlequin's newest series is going Hollywood!

Let us make you laugh with three months of terrific books, authors and romance, plus a chance to win a FREE 15-copy video collection of the best romantic comedies ever made.

For more details look in the back pages of any Love & Laughter title, from July to September, at your favorite retail outlet.

Don't forget the popcorn!

Available wherever
Harlequin books are sold.

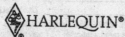

HARLEQUIN®

Look us up on-line at: http://www.romance.net

LLCELEB

Don't miss these Harlequin favorites by some of our most popular authors! And now you can receive a discount by ordering two or more titles!

HT#25700	HOLDING OUT FOR A HERO by Vicki Lewis Thompson	$3.50 U.S. ☐/$3.99 CAN.☐
HT#25699	WICKED WAYS by Kate Hoffmann	$3.50 U.S. ☐/$3.99 CAN.☐
HP#11845	RELATIVE SINS by Anne Mather	$3.50 U.S. ☐/$3.99 CAN.☐
HP#11849	A KISS TO REMEMBER by Miranda Lee	$3.50 U.S. ☐/$3.99 CAN.☐
HR#03359	FAITH, HOPE AND MARRIAGE by Emma Goldrick	$2.99 U.S. ☐/$3.50 CAN.☐
HR#03433	TEMPORARY HUSBAND by Day Leclaire	$3.25 U.S. ☐/$3.75 CAN.☐
HS#70679	QUEEN OF THE DIXIE DRIVE-IN by Peg Sutherland	$3.99 U.S. ☐/$4.50 CAN.☐
HS#70712	SUGAR BABY by Karen Young	$3.99 U.S. ☐/$4.50 CAN.☐
HI#22319	BREATHLESS by Carly Bishop	$3.50 U.S. ☐/$3.99 CAN.☐
HI#22335	BEAUTY VS. THE BEAST by M.J. Rodgers	$3.50 U.S. ☐/$3.99 CAN.☐
AR#16577	BRIDE OF THE BADLANDS by Jule McBride	$3.50 U.S. ☐/$3.99 CAN.☐
AR#16656	RED-HOT RANCHMAN by Victoria Pade	$3.75 U.S. ☐/$4.25 CAN.☐
HH#28868	THE SAXON by Margaret Moore	$4.50 U.S. ☐/$4.99 CAN.☐
HH#28893	UNICORN VENGEANCE by Claire Delacroix	$4.50 U.S. ☐/$4.99 CAN.☐

(limited quantities available on certain titles)

	TOTAL AMOUNT	$ _____
DEDUCT:	10% DISCOUNT FOR 2+ BOOKS	$ _____
	POSTAGE & HANDLING	$ _____
	($1.00 for one book, 50¢ for each additional)	
	APPLICABLE TAXES*	$ _____
	TOTAL PAYABLE	$ _____

(check or money order—please do not send cash)

To order, complete this form, along with a check or money order for the total above, payable to Harlequin Books, to: **In the U.S.:** 3010 Walden Avenue, P.O. Box 9047, Buffalo, NY 14269-9047; **In Canada:** P.O. Box 613, Fort Erie, Ontario, L2A 5X3.

Name: _____

Address: _____ City: _____

State/Prov.: _____ Zip/Postal Code: _____

*New York residents remit applicable sales taxes.
Canadian residents remit applicable GST and provincial taxes.

Look us up on-line at: http://www.romance.net

HBKJS97

HARLEQUIN SUPERROMANCE®

brings you
another

MARRIAGE OF
INCONVENIENCE

This September look for

MOTIVE FOR MARRIAGE (#755)
by Linda Markowiak

Nathan Perry has a perfect motive for marriage. He's going to
lose his young daughter for the second time unless he can
persuade Libby Jamieson, the woman who's about to adopt little
Sara, to marry him. Nate hasn't seen his daughter since she
was placed in a witness protection program with her mother—
Nate's ex-wife—and her stepfather. Now, eight years later,
Nate's ex and her husband are dead, and Sara's living with
Libby, who has known and loved the child for years.

Nate wants his child back. He wants to be a real father to her.
But his daughter loves Libby—and Nate is beginning to
understand her feelings. In fact, he's beginning to share them.

Available in September 1997
wherever Harlequin books are sold.

HARLEQUIN SUPERROMANCE®

There's more to the story...

For the very first time, award-winning authors

Leigh Greenwood

and

Peg Sutherland

have combined their unique talents
in a saga that spans two generations.

An unforgettable tale that proves once again
that true love really does conquer all!

Join us in the Old South for this outstanding story
of pride and passion!

ONLY YOU (#754)

Coming in September 1997

Look for *Only You* wherever Harlequin books are sold.